T0351435

SOLITARY

THE ITALIAN LIST

MAURIZIO TORCHIO

SOLITARY

■

Translated by Anne Milano Appel

LONDON NEW YORK CALCUTTA

SERIES EDITOR
Alberto Toscano

Seagull Books, 2019

Originally published in Italian as *Cattivi*, 2015
© Giulio Einaudi Editore S.p.A, 2015

First published in English translation by Seagull Books, 2019
English translation © Anne Milano Appel, 2019

ISBN   978 0 8574 2 607 9

British Library Cataloguing-in-Publication Data
A catalogue record for this book is available from the British Library

Typeset by Seagull Books, Calcutta, India
Printed and bound by WordsWorth India, New Delhi, India

The crippled, crippled. It's the crippled who believe in miracles. It's the slaves who believe in freedom.

Derek Walcott, *Dream on Monkey Mountain*

Thus the state is by nature clearly prior to the family and to the individual, since the whole is of necessity prior to the part: for example, if the whole body be destroyed, there will be no foot or hand, except in an equivocal sense, as we might speak of a stone hand . . . But he who is unable to live in society, or who has no need because he is sufficient for himself, must be either a beast or a god: he is no part of a state.

Aristotle, *Politics*

They bark: Ears. You bend your ears forward and turn around, first right, then left.

Nostrils. You tilt your head back to make the inspection easier.

Mouth. You open your mouth. The body's doorways open on command. You open your mouth but they don't feed you. They don't put something in: they check to see that you don't have anything.

Lift your tongue. You obey.

Stick out your tongue. You obey.

Gums. You move your lips aside, using your hands. Your fingers doing the guards' bidding.

Your mouth is empty, nothing irregular. Going back it's easy for it to be empty, because you have to talk a lot when you go on leave. You have to go to a woman who is familiar with prison: because she was locked up herself, or because she was brought to visit a father or a brother there as a child. Maybe her husband is still there. There are girls who are in a hurry and don't understand. They think that if you haven't seen a woman in twenty years, you'll want to get your fill when you're outside. Instead, a woman who knows prison will take you home, feed you drop by drop. You'll go there in the afternoon, hoping it will soon be dark. She'll offer you coffee.

And you'll talk. And talk. You have to empty your mouth. Let some of the prison out. If you don't talk, there's no room for anything else.

Toro goes to a woman like that.

Back in prison they order: Hands, and you hold out your arms, you spread your fingers, as if to keep from falling. Walking in the dark. Then you begin wiggling your fingers. Hard to know why. Who can manage to conceal something in the fingers of an open palm? But when you come back from a leave you're so proud of your hands that you're almost glad to do it. They're the hands of a man, finally. Would you like some coffee?, the woman must have asked. Thanks, Toro must have replied. You put the cup in your mouth and it feels like a sink between your lips, it's so thick, so weighty. I've never been let out on leave, nor will I ever be. But I experienced it when I got taken out to go to a trial eight years ago. A real teaspoon, of stainless steel, hard to stir with. The clinking, after years of plastic. If the cup falls, it breaks, you have a responsibility. It's a cup for adults. When the police escort you, they might stop at the auto-grill and buy you a cup of coffee. The guards never do. Because the cops are used to dealing with people who are free, not yet caught. They teach policemen to recognize a face, even after many years. Not the guards.

Armpits. Toro raises his arms.

Lifts and separates. Lifts his penis, separates his testicles.

A few hours before, the woman had held them in her hands, warm flesh replacing the prison's cold walls.

Toro more naked in front of the guards than in front of her.

In prison you relearn a fear of the dark. Toro probably asked her to turn on a small lamp, an abat-jour, and move it to the floor, under the bed. To put layers between them and the light. And in that dim glow they must have looked at each other. The woman, familiar with prison, doesn't apologize for how small the room is. She turns on the gas stove. Almost all the objects around them existed a good twenty years ago. Maybe not in that room. Maybe not exactly in those colors. Maybe bigger, less shabby, newer. But nothing around makes you uncomfortable. Since the woman turned off her cell phone and set it on the bedside table, nothing seems to come from the future. Nothing forces you to count the years. The yellow gleam from under the bed, the blue gleam of the gas stove.

The guys on the tiers look at women on television, see them on visiting days. I don't.

Okay, turn around, the guards snap.

Feet, they order. First one foot, then the other, like a horse. Feet immediately marked by prison.

Bend down and open up.

Toro crouches and spreads his thighs.

Cough.

If you don't cough from the cold, you cough on command. They do it to humiliate you. To really check they should use a scanner, or put on a glove, insert a finger. Instead, they make you bend over and cough, observing the contractions. An order is more forceful if it's pointless.

Fortunately, Toro is still suffused with the woman.

Each time, when they part, she blesses him. Like a son leaving for war. A sixty-year-old son.

And each time she asks him: Why don't you escape? You're serving life, why do you go back? But Toro knows that they would catch him immediately. In his neighborhood, at his bar, at the table in the back, the one near the wall.

The only ones who are truly able to escape are those who are capable of living anywhere: not calling, not writing. Not contacting anybody, ever. Dying in one place and being reborn in another, with no regrets. Moving the way money is moved: in a flash, without even seeing it. But Toro is someone who has always dealt in cash. He has hands that are big as shovels. The body of a man who has worked for generations, even though he's never worked. The only heavy stuff was the money, heaps of money. And the constant problem of finding satchels, suitcases, vaults, checkrooms, places able to hold all that money. Watching out for water, fire, animals, molds. Wind and rain. And being worried that you forgot a little of it, somewhere. And you can't remember where.

Toro isn't capable of vanishing.

For men like him, being on the lam means hiding in a bunker, underground, close to home. Near a son, buried close by.

Better off in prison: you see more sunlight, you meet more people.

That's why Toro left the woman and started walking, dodging cars and passers-by.

Outside there is always someone who crowds you, and the cars become more and more silent each year. Inside, even in the biggest prison, if you know who you are, you can get around. Someone like Toro can walk along with his eyes closed in here, because everyone will let him pass. A prison without an orderly walking area is a prison where no one wants to be. Here, when the first- or third-floor guys, who are organized, go down to get some air, the yard is orderly. When it comes to the second or the ground floor, it's a disaster, because they're all drug addicts or people who don't belong.

But outside nothing is organized: you have to side-step continually. You sense the haste of the individuals around you. You have the feeling that everyone is lined up behind you, and wondering: Who is that slow man? And sometimes it's true. You also have the impression they know where you're from. But that's never true, because those outside never think about the inside.

Yesterday Toro got to the station almost an hour early. Although this is his fourth leave, he's still unable to time himself, he's afraid of being late, afraid of getting lost. He doesn't know the city, but he likes it that way. It's nice to roam around a place where you've never had a wife, or a son, where you don't remember what stores were there before now. To walk where no one has ever looked for you. Where you don't have either enemies or friends, and have no idea who supplies the slot machines in the bars. Where you don't know which sidewalks fathers have picked their sons up from, howling, while shop-keepers roll down the shutters and people whisper behind windows; and the father carries the son's body in his arms and walk on, not knowing where to go. Surrounded by vacant lots.

Toro grew up in a town of single-story homes, at most two-story, left half-completed, the walls unplastered, because property is worthless and those who have anything of value keep it hidden.

Now he's happy to walk in this city with no empty lots, with its narrow streets and houses that have been restored a thousand times, the cars parked underground or inside the buildings.

At the station he remains standing, waiting.

We're good at waiting.

Then he gets on the train, which is noisy and filthy like the prison. The heating doesn't work, like in prison. The conductors in uniform. We like trains. A departure time, an arrival time. Someone else driving.

The guards know it.

They search for escapees in the stations. They pick them up in clusters, proud of having bought a ticket.

But Toro is not an escapee, and after an hour and a half he got off at the right stop, along a stretch of coast that has only three lights: the station below, down by the sea; the prison, a quarter of a mile up; and a town on the ridge. Around the station there are rocks, a stone quarry, and nothing else.

Toro walks from the station to the prison, on terrain that is as new to him as the city. There are no buses for the town, just for the prison, and only at visiting times. There are more people in the prison than in the town. People from the town use the highway that runs inland. If they have to get to the shore, they go elsewhere.

This was a reformatory, originally.

The town was built by juvenile offenders, a hundred years ago, along with the prison and the road.

A town for the guards, higher up than the prison, because it seemed right that way. No guards live there now or frequent the cafe; and if prisoners' family members stop to buy something, the shopkeepers treat them badly. But the year of construction is still carved on the cornerstones, hidden beneath the street signs, along with the name of the first warden of the reformatory.

They even collected signatures in the town. They say that at one time, from this stretch of coast that's now so dark, infinite stars could be seen. Now instead, the prison tints the sky orange for miles around, every night, all night. It sucks energy from the land and projects it elsewhere. The land is left barren. For ships offshore, for planes above, town and station vanish. Rather than a hundred houses, only the prison is visible. And anyone looking out the window on cloudy nights sees a milky orange that dampens the spirit.

But the prison was there initially. First the darkness, then the prison, then the town.

Toro rings the bell: It's Toro, I'm back from leave.

Okay, wait there.

In a big prison Toro would probably be a nobody. Here, on the other hand, at least until five years ago, when you talked about Toro and Commander, you talked about the entire prison. The rest were worthless: addicts, incoherent weirdos, screwballs. Then the N's arrived. But Toro is still Toro. Nevertheless, even for him ringing the bell isn't enough. A normal prisoner will wait an hour, Toro five minutes. But he still has to wait. Eight in the evening, the outside world is starting to have supper. For the prison, it's already the dead of night. Only the guards' cars are in the parking lot; useless because they have nowhere to go. They too will stay locked up, sleeping in a barrack or working a shift.

After the outside door clicks shut, Toro walks through the intermural zone. A concrete wall, taller than the roof, had been built around the old stone-and-brick reformatory. And in the no-man's-land between the prison and the wall, they planted even taller poles, with round floodlights on top, like fumaroles or impaled jellyfish, a quarter of a mile above the sea.

Toro walks along protected by a metal grille. Between the outside, where the world lives, and the inside, where we live, live the dogs. At one time this was where inmates who lowered themselves down from the prison landed when they fell. Because here they went on doing what they did a hundred years ago, knotting sheets together and rappelling walls. And just like a hundred years ago, something always went wrong at the last minute. The intermural area is a cemetery of legs. Dogs jog over that cemetery.

Toro continues on, from gate to gate, until he reaches the room where he undresses, crouches and does his best to cough.

That's enough, get up, the guard says.

But he goes on coughing. Toro suffers from inertia, like an oil tanker. Like the prison.

The guard rummages through his clothes, then hands them to him, one by one.

Get dressed.

The guard checks his shoes, the seam between the sole and the upper. New shoes that make his feet bleed. The guard empties Toro's bag on the table: cans, books, snacks, magazines, matches, writing paper. Paper can also be ordered at the commissary, but nobody wants it because it's white. There's the idea that writing in black on white recalls cell bars. Toro bought blue paper with a dolphin design on it for the boy who lives with him. Or something like that. I didn't see it. But in prison you don't need to see everything, because many things are repeated. If they aren't dolphins they'll be koalas. They would write on velvet, if they could. They want soft things. Silver spangles for the foam of the waves. Potato chips. Sweet carbonated drinks.

When you say kidnapping, however, people think of the guardian, the one who stays with the victim, day after day, night after night. The low man on the totem pole. And most of the time the one who stays with the kidnapped victim is a savage brute, a monster who comes from a desolate area, little more than a beast. A filthy, primitive man who puts his hands on a decent person. And leaves them there too long.

This is disturbing to everyone, even to criminals.

You kept a mother away from her children for seven months!, they told me.

Because the woman we kidnapped had two children, and the newspapers were always writing about it, even when it had nothing to do with anything. And it made an impression.

But I wasn't the one who decided to kidnap her. I didn't even know who she was. I just had to do a little transporting with my van, at the beginning. Most of all: the seven months didn't depend on me. An abduction may last two days, two months, two years. Nobody knows. Which is also the reason you can't find financiers anymore. Drugs, gambling, real estate—anything else is a better bet. Kidnappings occur only in the third world now: too much labor, too much uncertainty, too little return. Though I'm convinced that even here there must still be some involved in kidnapping; it might have died off as an industry but survived as an artisanal craft. At least as long as the rich remain accessible. When they're able to buy themselves faster legs, and an intelligence that's a thousand times more developed, then only a rich man will be able to get to another rich man. Not before. If abductions are no longer done now, it's because trust has disappeared. We had reached the point of calling and asking the family: Tell me how much you actually paid. To check how much money there really was to divvy up. Because no one trusted the other members of the group.

A group can't just get together for the duration of the abduction. You have to know those working with you quite well. Know the man before he was born, him and his family. Be certain that if he betrays you, an entire town will make him pay for it. Without trust, without a town, kidnappings can't be done. Once people start locking their doors, you can be sure that nothing can happen there anymore.

It's already light.

We're entering a season when what should wake you at dawn are small birds, and water running into the porters' buckets. Here, instead, there are gulls everywhere, constantly making the same racket: day, night, summer, fall. They don't talk to each other, they screech. They screech because they're frightened or because they think they've found food, or because another gull is about to mate with their companion. They couldn't care less about the sun's rising. The little birds, the ones that sing and eat breadcrumbs, are afraid of the gulls. Once I saw a gull crack a little bird's head with his beak. Then he left it there, without eating it.

Here we don't even have breadcrumbs for the birds, bread that's dry, light, airy. Here everything is oily, it comes confined in boxes, it's consumed in confinement. Tuna for the most part. I've been eating tuna for so long that I should be dead. Every Tuesday in summer, during even weeks, tuna for lunch and supper. Plus supper on Fridays. During odd weeks only for Friday supper. In winter only for lunch on Tuesday, during even weeks.

We ate tuna on the island as well. In twenty years I've eaten a ton of cans, without seeing a single one, because cans can be used to cut.

Maybe some destitute priest, in certain communities, also lives on tuna. Or children in orphanages.

But nobody spends his whole life in an orphanage.

And even priests, sooner or later, find a way to get invited to dinner.

No fresh fruit, so no one can hide it and let it ferment. But anything can ferment: rice, potatoes. People get drunk no matter what.

My stomach must be riddled with holes. Anyone who for twenty years has been eating meals that cost less than dog food should be nauseated and screaming in pain. Commander, on the island, bragged about it to the journalists: I spend less on meals for the inmates than on food for the dogs.

Still, it rankles me less now than it did twenty years ago. A person who spends countless years in prison at times remains young in some strange way. Regular meals, regular sleep, no responsibilities . . . You eat crap, but regularly.

Commander had his photograph taken with his two dogs. These dogs work for the prison administration, he said, and they have never committed a crime. It's normal for them to be treated better.

That was just fine with those reading the newspapers in those years. In fact, they would have fed *us* to the dogs to save even more.

Commander told the reporters: I'm like these dogs. In the world there are sheep, dogs and wolves. The sheep are incapable of violence. He said: We wardens resemble wolves more so than sheep. We are trained in violence but, unlike wolves, we have chosen good.

The journalists nodded.

In this prison, of those who experienced the island, only Toro, Commander and I remain. Up until five years ago there was also Martini, but he's out now, he lives with a teacher.

Commander was brilliant as a young man. He was *already* a commander. Now he's *still* only a commander, and not for long.

He was truly convinced that he was in command. He seemed like a coiled spring, loaded toward a future where he would command even more. Who did I think I was?, he asked me one night, when he still came down to see me. I'm not ashamed of the things I did, because I did them thinking I was someone else. Who did I think I was?

Commander dictated to reporters: Here there are the worst of the worst.

They believed him. Even we believed him. He gave us pride. We looked at one another, at the sorry state we were in. There couldn't be more than twenty, maybe thirty worst of the worst . . . there were four hundred of us. But after a while we convinced ourselves that we were all the worst of the worse, no exclusions. The elite, the academy of crime. The most important place to end up: the nightmare in the spotlight. Not a small provincial jail like this one. It's easy to transform an island into the prison of prisons. It immediately has an effect. People feel safer if the worst are put in the middle of the sea.

It doesn't matter that you can fly by air, sail through water, and that the island is less than ten miles from the coast. Those at home think of how deep the sea is, and that the worst are there and will not return. They look at the photo of the cliffs, the mountain, arid, not a tree, the summit shrouded in fog. There were also olive trees, on the east side, and they stretched almost to the sea. But no one could photograph the island. And in the photos that Commander chose, there were never any olive trees.

As for food, they made the most of us on the island.

Whenever a new batch of prisoners came from the mainland, the first thing they did was take away their dentures. Then they gave them very little water and shitty food. In the span of a week, the bosses, who were almost all of a certain age, were transformed into a bunch of old men. You read it in the eyes of the other guys, of the young ones, of Toro: up until the day before they obeyed in terror and now, suddenly, they merely felt embarrassed. Terror had shifted from the bosses to the island: what was this island, which in one week had managed to reduce them to that? You just had to stop watering them, and all the leaves dropped off. The young guys wondered: Can we still obey toothless men? And the bosses lost weight. Having to mash up the food ruined the appetite more than the shitty food. Afterwards, even if the dentures are returned, it's not the same anymore because you know that they can take them away again, smash them at any time, with any excuse.

They broke all my teeth, but I never asked for dentures, and there's nothing I can't eat. You just have to use your gums. It just takes time. Time toughens anything.

Dentures are a weapon in the hands of the administration. You're more independent without them. Naturally, the sound of a voice with teeth is better, sure, it gives the impression you're thinking clearly. Inside my head, I still hear my voice with teeth. But to those outside I know it doesn't sound like that. It's like when you hear your voice recorded and you don't recognize it.

On the island, after the attempted breakout, the guards started pissing in the pots.

I didn't see them, because I was already down in the basement, but the others saw them every day. They put on a fine show, near the kitchen windows. They whipped it out of those coarse, ugly dark-blue pants. And they peed in our food.

During that time they had barred any extra food, seized the camping stoves. Everyone had to eat from the piss-fouled cart or starve to death. When it became known on the mainland, and the scandal broke, they stopped pissing. The newspapers wrote plenty about the island, always too late, but they wrote. The guards stopped pissing and did worse. They called in a nutritionist, a specialist who taught those idiots to make punitive bread like they did in other countries. I say idiots because, at that time, the guards were more ignorant than we were. And in fact a revolt was triggered. We had put up with everything: the fake firing squads, the banning of conversation, the beatings and piss in the soup. But not bread.

Punitive bread is a bread that isn't bread; it doesn't smell like bread even when it's freshly baked. Designed to keep you alive without ever being pleasurable.

Because even the stalest, moldiest discarded loaves, if you're hungry, provide something. You can save it, give it away, sell it. Eat it all at once or a little at a time. Not punitive bread. Among the cells, we swap everything. Even a fly can have value, if there is someone who raises spiders, maybe down the corridor, maybe on another floor: you pass the fly from cell to cell, from hand to hand, to where it can be useful. Not that bread. That thing wasn't human. Or maybe it was deviously human. It represented the ability to make the worst by putting together ingredients that, taken individually, are innocent: powdered milk, potatoes, carrots, tomato sauce, chopped meat, lard, flour, celery and beans. Yet combined intentionally, baked purposefully, they turned into a soggy, brick-colored thing that smelled of vomit, tasted like vomit, and was both insipid and greasy, overbaked and underbaked. A bread to be eaten like animals do, standing up, away from the table.

Punitive bread in other countries is only given to those in isolation. And even at that, the guards have to go in threes to bring it there, in anti-riot gear with shields to protect themselves.

Giving punitive bread to an entire prison is like setting fire to it.

Still, I don't hold a grudge against the man who tried to take away our pleasure in bread. He may still be alive somewhere, retired. If I were to meet him I would say hello. It's myself I can't forgive. The crap I ate, outside, of my own volition . . . Warm wine in cartons.

Because I was eating badly even before I came to prison, in my twenty-five years as a free man.

Especially during the kidnapping.

It's all written down.

They attached the list of items to the proceedings. The police had catalogued what they found inside the hideout, and even what was outside, in the plastic bags that I tied closed and threw a distance away, thinking that the woods were big, and that we would have to stay there forever to fill the ravine. I liked the idea. Staying there until that dark gap turned into an expanse of plastic and garbage. A uniform sea of plastic and garbage. Our stench. Not biodegradable.

I think they were mainly looking for evidence that we had had relations. Because that's the first thing everyone wonders about when the kidnapped victim is a woman. Did they have relations?

And they're right to wonder. Because they almost always have.

Instead, in our case they mostly found shit, along with plastic dishes and utensils, and used tea bags, given how damn cold it was. And towels cut into strips that she used as sanitary pads because I had forgotten to have them buy them. And tin cans. A heap of tin cans. Just like in prison, only there they were visible.

It could have been a nice summer. Instead, we always had an uneasy burning sensation in our stomachs. We wiped our mouths with our hands, and our hands with sheets of newspaper. The hideout was full of ants. The fine weather, wasted like that. For what?

Only in September did I begin to ask her: What do you want to eat?

They never ask me, and good thing, because I didn't ask often.

There were abductions in the city, where the kidnappers made love under silk covers, nice and warm, drinking champagne. We only hugged each other once. Hidden like rats, under the roots of the trees.

During these twenty years of imprisonment, I've met a lot of people. People just passing through, or people with life sentences.

Almost all of them have told me: I ruined a summer too, and I can't understand why. To punish ourselves? What for?

Except for someone who ended up inside too young, a juvenile maybe, but if a person has been able to live outside for five or six years, as an adult . . . When I describe how I threw away that summer, the other guy says: Me too. It was all there, and instead I wasted it.

At the beginning I didn't even want to go and get water.

In areas where kidnappings occur, going to get water is dangerous: the police know where the sources are. There are few places, because the areas are generally poor and barren, so every now and then the cops choose a water-hole and wait for the fugitive. A territory can be immense, but if it has only three water sources it's easy to monitor. Ours, however, was not an abduction zone. And it wasn't arid either. True, it was rocky and littered with stones. If you tried to pull up a fistful of earth, you found stones in it. Maybe that's why nobody cultivated it. It was full of worms, and molds. Woods and ravines. Dead leaves, all year long. You slid down. The woods became gorges, and at the bottom of the slopes there were rivulets of water. And no police.

They'd told me: Don't ever go out, don't leave her by herself.

They were keeping an eye on me from a distance, I'm sure of it. They were afraid I'd fall for her, and let her go. Nevertheless, they left me there alone just so they wouldn't have to pay someone else. Or maybe they lost faith in that kidnapping right away, and were content to stay out of it as much as possible.

One day a week I went to an old stable, a ten-minute walk from the hideout, and waited. Sometimes they came, sometimes they didn't. A small stable, maybe it had held a donkey, maybe three goats, back when animals roamed around those ravines. When the other guys came they brought two twenty-liter jerrycans. For everything. If we washed more, we had to drink and cook less.

Water is heavy. For nearly three months I made do. I couldn't leave her alone. And I was afraid of getting lost.

Usually they pick someone local to guard the victim. But I had never been to that area. It's absurd, it's one of the many absurd things about that time. They didn't trust anybody else, so they asked me, though I had never been involved in a kidnapping and was only supposed to transport the target. There was a state highway, a network of local roads, and a big barren area in the center. Over sixty square miles of nothing. And we were there, beyond the edge of the road, in the woods.

I was used to nature. From the van you see the sky for many hours, the clouds, you hear the rain beating on the roof. There are some jobs where you are overwhelmed by nature. You see maintenance men continually cutting back and repaving, to keep the underbrush and vegetation from eating up the highway. Trees all around full of huge nests, one every hundred yards. I don't think there are that many nests in the woods. Certainly not where we were. Maybe birds prefer highways: open space, a wide road, a runway where fledglings can fly, instead of a maze of tangled branches.

With the arrival of the heat, I began disobeying. When the jerrycan was empty I wrapped it in a plastic bag and went out: a white bag because the can was blue and it would have been too noticeable in the woods where the green tended to gray, and the trunks of the trees were almost white, and even the soil was pale.

I don't know the names of trees, I don't know much about the outdoors. I know that all the vivid colors were in the hideout.

We slept on inflatable air mattresses, in red and blue vinyl. The only ones that existed at that time. Inflated at the beginning of the night, nearly deflated by morning.

We used blue plastic mats as a floor covering. We even attached them to the earthen layer above us, which acted as a ceiling, so that it wouldn't rain in, and so ghastly critters wouldn't drop on our heads. A green military tarp covered the mouth of the cave.

The hideout was a hollow dug into the side of the ravine and lined with plastic. It smelled of plastic, the same whiff I smelled at the sea, as a child, when I stored the rubber dinghy in the cabin.

When I came back from the stream I could smell the plastic even before I entered. Besides our odor, naturally.

Coming from outdoors, as soon as I moved the tarp aside, it knocked the breath out of me.

But that was all right. What mattered was that she was still there, waiting for me.

I brought the water, and then I turned around while she washed.

She asked me to turn around and I did.

I could have made her wash my feet.

I only started thinking about it years later, reading a book, the diary of a nobleman, centuries ago, who walked all day and whose favorite time was in the evening when his maid would wash his feet. And I realized what an idiot I'd been. I threw away my happiness. There are no laws that forbid you from having your feet washed. They wouldn't have given me a single day more in prison if I had asked her, politely, every night to heat up some water and wash my feet. There are an infinite number of legal things that don't cost a thing but that improve life. We could have massaged one another for hours. We both had a lot of aches and pains. The hideout was damp. I've been in cells below sea level, but none that were ever so dank. We woke up and found the tarpaulins steaming from our breath. Literally dripping. Big drops. The vapor of our breaths, mine and hers mixed together, rained on us as we breathed at night. The breath that you don't see as it keeps you alive was there, on the ceiling, a few inches from us, in drops bigger than any natural rain. And it dripped back on us. Soaking us and the sleeping bags. And we knew that the few days of sunshine would not be able to dry us out, because in the woods the rays struggled to get through the leaves. We shivered until we couldn't breathe and then she'd ask me to please move aside the tarp covering the entrance a little, to let some fresh air in.

Because she couldn't get there.

The chain was purposely measured so that she couldn't reach that far. There's some idea that a hostage shouldn't see anything of the outside world, because afterward he could lead the police to the hideout. And in the hideout the police always find something. In a place where you've lived for so long, there are always lots of traces that can be introduced at trials. On the day of liberation it's not as if you can light a bonfire, and send everything up in flames. You have to slip away quietly, like a ghost. That's why it's important that the hostage not know where he is.

I've never put much stock in it.

From the mouth of the cave you could see the ravine and the woods, nothing more. A sliver of a mountain. But it was a mountain that lacked any particular signs. Not even I knew what it was called. Even if they showed her photos of mountains, once freed, they wouldn't include that one. It wasn't an abduction zone. It wasn't an important mountain. It was a mountain with a clean record, so to speak. Maybe it wasn't even a real mountain.

There was nothing really wild about the place where we were, as uninhabited as it was. Nothing majestic. Far removed from civilization. It looked like a section of woods in a neighborhood of row houses, forgotten by the bulldozers only because it was too steep.

Nonetheless, I didn't let her look out at first.

I was the one who crawled over on all fours, without getting out of the sleeping bag. I moved the tarp aside and held it open with a rock. Most of the time it was dark and foggy out there.

We slept in our clothes. Until May or June. It's cold in the woods, far from cities and towns. Far from shepherds' pastures, far from hunting trails.

Then I started to sleep in my underwear. But I kept my pants in the sleeping bag with me and put them on before I came out.

When the heat arrived, we decided to leave the entry tarp always open, even though it got light early and the brightness woke us up. Animal noises also woke us up.

The animals made embarrassing sounds. The entire woods were fucking, and we kept quiet, thinking the same thing: about all those nameless animals who crowded around us and kept us from speaking, but also from remaining silent peacefully.

She had never slept in a tent. She was one of those girls who, at seventeen, on their first vacation without parents, go to a hotel with a girlfriend. Like two old ladies.

She asked me for earplugs. I had them. A kidnapper always has earplugs for the hostage to wear. But after an hour she took them out, because the earplugs couldn't make her forget the noise that, outside, continued.

One night the wind released the tarp from the rock; the tarpaulin fell shut, the wind died down, and we woke up sealed in and thoroughly drenched, with no air. Then, in my underpants, I went to open up the tarp. It was still dark. And she too came out of her sleeping bag, saying: It's stifling. And we stayed that way, sitting on the sleeping bags. We waited for the sun, legs crossed.

Had breakfast, pretending not to notice. She in her underwear and chain. I in my underwear and balaclava.

And I kept looking at her, from behind my black wool ski-mask.

The balaclava is the only garment that you can never ever remove, for whatever reason.

If it accidentally falls off, you have to kill those around you. The kidnapped victims know it. They know that a balaclava that falls off is like a pistol shot. That's why they're the first to encourage you to put it on right.

The only difference between a hood for kidnappers and one for hostages is that the one for victims has no eye holes.

You can keep a hostage constantly in the dark. Constantly hooded and wearing earplugs. Drip wax in his ears, burst his eardrums. Lock him in a cellar with no windows. Alternatively, you can take a chance, cover yourself instead, be careful what you say. And let him experience the light, the seasons, life. It's the difference between heaven and hell. Even if he has only the wall of a cave to look at, even if you tell him, Never turn toward the opening for any reason, or I'll kill you ... well ... He still has a whole world to himself. Where things happen. Ants, spiders, flies, damp spots; things that change, expand, dry up, move around. The sun especially. Time passes. You can adapt. It can become *your* world, *your* refuge. You can survive. One can adapt to anything. Only in darkness and silence can you not. They aren't human, they never will be. Like deep space, or a coffin.

I, as a jailer, never inflicted darkness.

It's one of the things I'm most proud of.

It's one of the things that should guarantee you a reduced sentence. But they never ask you that, at trials.

What matters is how much you cooperate, not what you did. If you repent, if you sell someone out . . . you can get anything you want. Otherwise you stay here and rot. It never even occurs to lawyers, judges, law makers. It doesn't occur to the kidnapped victim either. It only occurs to someone who has known darkness.

A few years ago, here in prison, I was chatting with a man who was involved in the kidnapping of an old man.

After a while, you always end up talking about crimes and trials.

He told me that they held the old man underground, in a cellar with no windows. The only light came from an electric bulb that they had attached to a car battery. As long as the battery lasted, the light was always on. They passed by once a week. If the battery died before they got there, the hostage remained in the dark. One day, after five months, a miracle happened. I wouldn't know what else to call it. A little bird managed to get down there, to the old man's tomb. The guy who told me about it didn't know how the bird had done it. Maybe he'd flown in as they were opening the door for the weekly drop by, but there were still two doors to pass through . . . In any case, it doesn't matter. The old man told him that at some point he found himself with this little bird on his shoulder. When he told him about it, the bird was already dead. I had to kill him, the old man said. I couldn't take the chance that, for some reason, he might peck at the bulb, or cause it to fall. The last time I was in the dark for three days, before you came. I couldn't take it.

I mean, you imagine a great story of friendship, the little bird eating from the old man's hand and singing for him, things like that, and instead. He killed him almost immediately. No regrets. He broke the bird's neck. Just not to risk it.

Imposing darkness and silence is a despicable choice.

That's where the real difference between cruelty and humanity lies. But maybe I'm no better. Maybe if we had kidnapped an old man, I too would have kept him hooded, in the dark, underground.

Her, on the other hand—I wanted to look at her. I was willing to put up with my sweat, my salt, stinging my eyes, just to see her exposed face. The whole time.

Except when she asked me to turn around, so she could wash, and I, like a fool, turned around.

The helicopters only flew over once.

From before dawn until late at night.

We heard the police dogs barking on the other side of the gorge. Me and her, filthy, with our odor. What if they come here? she asked. I'll start shooting, I told her. And I released the safety catch on the gun. I didn't know how to shoot, I can't shoot, I've never fired a shot. But you always have to say that: If they come, we'll all die. That way the hostage won't scream, won't call out. He becomes a child and falls silent. You create intimacy. What unites you is not the fact that the hostage can do nothing and you everything. On the contrary. The hostage knows that the kidnapper is weaker than he is, in certain respects. He knows that the first bullet, when the police arrive, will be for the kidnapper. But he also knows that bullets sometimes go wherever they want. This brings them together. The immense power of fear, out there. And us in here, weak.

In the evening, when the helicopters had gone, she took my hand. She didn't say that at the trial, and good thing, because they wouldn't have understood. She, the mother of a family, ventured to hold my hand. And she judged me right, because all I really did was hold her hand, even after she fell asleep, and I heard the blood pounding in my ears so loud that I was afraid: would the cops up there in the helicopters hear it too? Loud enough to make them come back.

From that night on we never stopped talking to each other. But we hardly ever touched. The smaller a place is, the less you brush against each other by accident. You learn to respect people's space, like here. If someone brushes against you it's because he means to. We touched on the night of the helicopters, and the last days when I taught her to walk again. Also on the very first day, when she suddenly raised a hand toward the hood and I stopped her wrist, for fear that she would take it off. She had to ask my permission to straighten her hair. I decided she could do it, and use her hand.

Sometimes we talked all night too, like you do in prison. The emptier a place is, the more you fill it with words.

At first I had to give her the speech you always give, especially if you let the hostage stay without a hood: You have to try to hear and see as little as possible. Because afterwards the police will question you for days, they won't give you a moment's peace. Those guys are heartless.

Like you people, she said.

Like us. And if you have anything to tell them, and you tell them, we'll be forced to come looking for you and your family. And you'll never forgive yourself. Then I added: I work with people who will stop at nothing. I added that because I suspected she was already beginning to feel less afraid of me.

Consequently, she didn't speak much until the day of the helicopters.

After that, it was I who forced myself to only listen. Once when she was in a particularly good mood, she complained, joking: What! We've been living together for almost three months and I still don't know anything about you . . . And when she realized what she had said she put her hand over her mouth. She was scared. Because harmless things that are said in the woods can be repeated in the city, at the trials. Or they can force you to kill, to prevent that.

Our lives depended on her not knowing anything about me.

When I really couldn't keep my mouth shut, I made things up. I invented a family. You already have a son?, she asked, surprised. Thinking she hadn't yet noticed how young I was, I turned red under the balaclava. I didn't know anything about kids. I only knew my sister's daughter, recently born at the time. Now I know even less. Now, if I met a child, I would look at him the way you look at a Martian. Because every now and then you see a woman even here in the isolation hole. But a child, no, never, only at visitation. I was twenty-five when they arrested me. The N's at twenty-five already have a pack of kids. Those who come from a family, a street or a neighborhood accustomed to prison, take into account the possibility of a life sentence and have kids right away, so that the stock will continue and the children can come on visitation days and talk to them on the phone. Those familiar with prison know that they should have kids without delay, between one sentence and another, as long as the sentences are still short. And you have to have a lot of kids, because someone will kill them on you.

For me it was different.

I never had a relative in prison.

When I was arrested and then sentenced to thirty years, I thought: With a little good conduct I'll be out in twenty years, and at forty-five you can still have a lot of kids, if you want . . . Then I killed the guard, and they gave me life without possibility of parole. They enter 99/99/9999 into the computers, because computers need a definite term. Life is something a computer can't understand. Kids are something I can't understand.

During the kidnapping, when I said I missed my invented kid, it wasn't true, but when I said I missed my invented wife it was true, because I imagined *her*, that woman who had never gone camping, as a wife.

You always end up saying something that's true, when you talk. Those who don't talk to their hostages have good reason not to. Still, a person can sometimes take a lot of precautions and then the hostage will hear an airplane pass by, and as the plane passes church bells ring out, and as chance would have it the hostage is an avid aviation buff who is able to recognize a plane by the sound of its engine, and it turns out that that particular type of military aircraft takes off from only one airport in the entire country. And afterwards, thanks to the timing of the church bells and the flight plans, they can reconstruct the exact distance between the hideout and the airport, and discover the hideaway.

It's rotten luck, of course, but it has happened. How can you foresee every little thing?

I mean, really: either you keep people in a well, stuffed with sleeping pills, or you might as well talk.

However, if you stuff a hostage with sleeping pills, you run the risk that he might die.

I went too far in the opposite direction, but I don't regret it.

At one point I was sweating so much in the balaclava that scratching myself made my skin flake.

So she suggested: Let's take turns at night. Every other night you put the hood on me, and you can breathe. She was kind.

I refused.

I took it off for a couple of hours, when it was darker.

You had to remember not to light a cigarette, at those times.

You had to wait for the moon to go down.

I was in a corner.

But a little brightness came in just the same every now and then.

You could make out the white of the underwear, of the eyes. Also one of the books I'd brought her, which had a white cover: sometimes you could tell where it was.

And there was a chance I'd fall asleep. She swore to me that she would warn me. She swore to me that, in any case, if she woke up and saw light through her eyelids, she would ask: Are you covered up? Can I open my eyes? And she did that, a couple of times. And I believe she was sincere.

But how can you, when you just wake up, and you're coming out of your dreams, how can you remember where you are, who you're with, remember that you're sleeping beside a man you can't look at?

At least a couple of times I woke up and it was already light and she was sleeping. Or pretending to be asleep.

I don't care. Given the way it later ended up, I might as well not have worn the hood the whole time. Told her all about me. We might as well have looked at each other face to face.

Modesty is a weird thing.

On the island they discovered that in-house relocations went more smoothly if they made us strip. A naked prisoner, in general, has less desire to stop and chat, or pick a quarrel with the guards. He's in more of a hurry to get where he's going. And we're talking about the same prisoner who shits in a Turkish toilet, in the cell, in front of everybody. But there's nothing you can do about it, some things you never really get used to. Even time labors over some things.

In theory, you shouldn't hang a curtain between the toilet's low wall and the ceiling, because it would block the guards' visual control. On the island, for example, they didn't allow us to. Here they do. But anyway, curtain or no curtain, you're still shitting in the middle of a room full of people. Whenever someone goes to the bathroom, and someone else is forced to smell it, they all remember that basically they aren't men, that they're not free. That Turkish toilet in the middle of the room makes each of us the other's persecutor, every time. Maybe that's why you then go to sleep in your pajamas, even if it's hot. And shower in your underpants.

Only the guards shower in the nude. The guards have no shame, or dignity. This is a level prison, a rectangle made of two long sides facing one another: the guards' building and the inmates' building. Two short sides, as connecting passages. Plus an opening in the middle, which is the yard, long and narrow, like a third building without a roof. In the new prisons, the guards can see the detainees whenever they want, through surveillance cameras, and the prisoners almost never see them. Here, instead, you could hang clothes to dry from one building to another, like in a tenement. And everyone sees the guards go out in the corridor naked, vomiting, chasing one another around. With no curtains. They live in filth. The barracks are the filthiest place in the whole prison. Any porter can confirm it: they'd rather clean the addicts' showers than the guards' dormitory.

Then again, I'm not that big on cleanliness either.

I try not to forget that this isn't a house, it's a cell. It's not even *my* cell, it's *a* cell. I keep it a little dirty. Not as filthy as the guards, but not perfectly spotless either. I would be entitled to a plastic mirror and a razor, because I'm not considered at risk, but I didn't want them. The showers don't have hot water, so I don't go overboard with bathing, just as I don't look after the cell too much. This is not my home, this is no longer my body. I don't wash much and I look at myself as little as possible. Not to get confused. I don't want to start imagining that I'm really talking to a woman when I talk to the nurse once a day. That if I shake hands with a female lawyer I'm touching a woman. It's not the same thing. It's no longer my hand.

The uncertainty that you might have some residual good looks can disturb your tranquillity.

Not much, but it can disturb it. Even a guard told me so, one day, on the way to the shower: Why don't you try to get out, you're still a good-looking guy. Why don't you have them give you a denture?

The uncertainty of having missed an opportunity ... That's why I hide under the blankets whenever someone walks past the heavy cell door.

When she began asking me about the ransom, I told her: It's no use, I don't know. It's not my job. But I said it in an odd tone, like someone who knows things and doesn't want to say. In fact, she didn't believe me, and I was pleased about that.

Until one evening—one of the first nights we were eating in the dark again, now that summer was over, looking out of the mouth of the cave as if we were sitting on a little balcony—one evening I leaned over to her and whispered: We demanded twenty billion for you.

I whispered it to her, because it was a breath-taking figure.

An unheard-of sum. I mean, there have been some who started off at fifty billion but then quickly backed down to seven. Because sometimes kidnappers are incompetents, people who make it up as they go along. I told her twenty billion because, to me, she was worth it. For less, I would not have given her back to those two children she was always talking about, and to that husband she never talked about. It was my way of paying her a compliment. How much are you worth? A lot. You're worth a whole lot, you're worth more than anyone who has ever been kidnapped. You're my treasure. How many years must a person work, usually, to earn twenty billion? Ten lifetimes? A hundred? For me, you're worth all of them.

I was young, all talk. It was like offering her a huge bouquet of flowers.

She, however, turned pale.

She said: We're not that type of family. We don't have that kind of money. You chose wrong.

I told her: Your father is the Coffee King.

Right after the abduction the newspapers had heralded: 'Coffee King's Daughter Kidnapped.' The family members were furious and demanded a media blackout, because headlines like that drive the ransom up. But I didn't know anything about the press's silence. For me, she was still the Coffee Princess.

She told me: Until fifteen years ago all we had was a big coffee-roasting plant. Now we have thirty employees, but our coffee is still only distributed locally. Some in the main town . . . If you go much more than fifty miles away there isn't a single cafe that has our brand.

Then she looked down, her shoulders slumped and she crumpled up like a dried leaf. We aren't that kind of people, she said again.

I wanted to tell her: That's why I couldn't find your coffee, the day I went to town. I planned to make you your coffee the next morning, as a surprise. I didn't know it was only served in coffee bars. And only miles away from here.

I wanted to admit: Anyway, I was joking, see? I don't know anything.

Tell her: You think I'm all-powerful, because I'm always watching you, and I have a gun, and I dictate what you should write home. But I dictate the things that others write for me, reading from a sheet of paper. And I don't know how to use the gun.

Instead I was firm: Until they pay, we keep you here.

Money or time.

That's always the way: money or time.

If you don't pay with money, you pay with time. Or with your life, which is the same thing.

Here they assign you a flight risk based on how much money you've managed to set aside, outside. Also based on previous escape attempts, on how agile, resourceful, bold or desperate you are, but chiefly based on money. If you have money, there will be a lot of people eager to free you, to share it with you.

Here they haven't even installed a grille over the exercise yard.

They take it for granted that nobody will ever come to get us out. And they're wrong, if you ask me, because it's one thing to be poor, but how can you rule out the fact that a woman might fall in love, get a pilot's license, procure a weapon, hijack a helicopter for you, do it all by herself? Fly hundreds of miles, risk a hundred years in jail, to come and liberate a worthless prisoner . . . Rescue him from the sky. It's happened before, elsewhere, it could also happen here.

Anyway, after the Coffee Princess' response, when I went to the old stable to get the provisions I said: We got it all wrong. The organizer screwed us up. I'd like to know what he saw, what he made up. This woman has never even heard the word billions! For her, billions are what they are for me, or for you, something absurd, incalculable. They're a nation's treasury, or snowflakes on a mountain. They won't be able to pay. They'll never be able to pay.

And what I meant was: Not just the twenty billion I made up, they won't be able to pay the billions you're demanding either.

How do you know that?, the supplier interrupted me.

Then he threatened me. He said that I had been alone with her for too long. I was losing my ability to see things clearly, and he would pass it on. Maybe they would send someone to relieve me.

I froze.

They all deny it, all of them!, he added. You could kidnap the richest man in the world, and both he and his family would weep and swear to you that you were mistaken. But in the end they pay. The Coffee King will pay up too. Now go back there and cut off her ear.

At that point I realized that the supplier was not just a supplier. He had to be important to give orders like that.

Don't think they reason like you do, he told me, because if they reasoned like you they wouldn't have money. Those people negotiate, they negotiate to the death. They try to get the price down. If the family pays right away, the kidnapped victim is the first to get upset, because it means they're squandering money that is also his, they're mortgaging his future, for what? For a stupid month or two less away from home.

People are disturbed by sliced-off ears, the supplier concluded. But they're just pieces of cartilage with no nerves. It hurts no more than getting them pierced for an earring. The important thing is to disinfect the wound thoroughly, before and after. Give her antibiotics. Change the bandage often. Then, when she's free again, if she doesn't like it she'll have it fixed. The money she wouldn't give us, she'll give to a surgeon.

He was right. I mean, I don't know if she had her ear fixed, but cutting it off worked, it reduced the time of her captivity. Cutting off an ear is one of the few intelligent things kidnappers do. She understood, and she didn't complain.

There was a time when I too would have willingly cut off a limb, to get out early.

Or I would have had myself injected with something that would suddenly make me old, like those kids who, at eight, look like they're seventy, and who at thirteen are already dead. Because if the punishment is to grow old, then you might as well do it in a hurry. Save yourself money, boredom, suffering. How much is a hand worth? I would have accepted it. Accepted having a stump, but outside. With life without parole, however, there aren't enough limbs to pay the price. You have to keep all your arms and legs, even if they're of no use in here, and are more or less a farce.

She hated to write home.

She cried for hours, afterwards.

They told me: Make her write this, and this, and then put in something of her own, some reminiscence. But warn her that if she adds a message in code, we'll kill her and scatter her parts in the woods.

A lot of them were obsessed with the idea of flinging the pieces into the woods.

Some really did it, even with those who paid. They figured: A dead man can't talk, let the feral pigs eat him!

And they risked ruining us, because people aren't fools, especially the wealthy. After they pay a few times, and nothing comes of it, they start to think that it may be better to adopt a hard line, stop the payments and let the law handle it.

Obviously only a few gangs behaved that way, but the damage was general. They couldn't manage to look beyond their hostage, their trial. They were people who performed abductions already thinking about the aftermath, about when they would be arrested, and worried only about that.

The organizer who hired me wasn't like that. He threatened to feed her to the wild boars to scare her, and

I didn't even repeat it to her. On the contrary, I said: Don't be afraid, if you don't try to run away, we won't harm you. Then I told her to think of a trusted friend to whom to address the letter. A friend who wasn't too obvious, though. Someone the police may not have already put under surveillance. The classic friend whom you haven't seen for years, but if you meet him, it's as if only a day has gone by. He has to be clever, this man or woman, and courageous, to succeed in delivering the letter into your father's hands. And also kind-hearted, because in any case you're dragging him into trouble.

You think about your contacts in a new way, to assign such a responsibility. You consider your friendships, one by one. At a certain point, the Princess lit up and said: Her! Of course, her! How could I not have thought of her right away? And she told me about that friend, and how they came to know each other, and how foolish they'd been not to see each other anymore.

We used three different intermediaries during those two hundred and twenty-one days. Two women and a male friend. All three, we later learned, had gone to the police first thing.

It's typical. She had written, begging them not to. But they hadn't been able to distinguish her voice from ours. Which was what made the Princess cry. That sheet of paper is the only opening to a world that was once yours, that is now light-years away, and that must include all of us: rape victim and kidnappers, bound closely together. Along with the eyes of the police. Because ultimately, or even from the beginning, everything ends with the police. Neither the victims, nor the families, are able to recover the letters: at most, a censored copy, years later, once the trial is over.

If nothing else, the Princess talked to me. It's worse for hostages forced to remain silent. They imagine those letters, day after day. They spend weeks writing them, inside their heads, they're the only words available to them. Then, when the time comes, the kidnappers distort them, or don't deliver them. Or those at home don't believe them. The most sincere, most important words of their lives, mistaken for their abductor's words.

Dissected by the police.

Over the years, as long as my mother was still alive, I always wrote to her. Some mothers only learn to read and write when a son goes to prison, so they can learn what's become of him from the newspapers, from letters, from trial proceedings. Not my mother. My mother was fairly brilliant: greeting cards and condolences were always written by her, for the entire family. But when she wrote to me in prison, she became lackluster. Always the same things. I knew how much those empty phrases had cost her. How much shame, how much privacy. She must have had to pull them out forcefully, a visceral extraction. Wishing Happy Easter to someone who's incarcerated is more difficult than transcribing your dreams for another person. She was embarrassed. My mother was ashamed to write: Everyone sends their regards, or: Your little niece is getting big.

I could see the shame that lay behind the words before they came to me.

I responded mainly to reassure her: I'm fine.

And I knew that the hands that held me prisoner would open the letter first.

The Coffee Princess did not write to reassure anyone.

She had to make them worry.

Light a fire under them! Make them feel guilty, let your father know how bad things are, that time is running out: something is about to break, inside, and it can't be fixed. That even if you come home, you'll never be the same again. Write that you won't be able to love them anymore.

And I hoped for that.

Put in some details, so that at home they'll feel awful. It's in your interest. And ours.

Write how much you miss them. Write that you're proud of the children, but disappointed in your father, and you can't believe that they've abandoned you. Add some family tradition, some custom you've had, some silly little thing that you've done every year since you were a kid, that this year you might not be able to do. Maybe never again. Because if they continue collaborating with the police, either you'll kill yourself or we'll kill you.

Really?, she asked.

No, I told you. If you don't try to run away, sooner or later you'll go home.

Writing the words she put together infuriated her.

She wept. She said: It's not true. She said: Forcing me to lie is the ultimate freedom you're taking from me.

It made me think: Oh, so you're not so bad off! Say it. You don't have to write it. Just say it to me, in this hole dug in the ground, halfway down a ravine. Tell me: I'm okay hidden here, with you. If I write to my parents that things are bad here, I'm lying.

Sometimes I had to rush her.

I wasn't warned in advance either. I knew nothing about the negotiations. When they needed a letter they didn't wait for our contact day. They came to the hideout, unexpectedly, called me outside, then waited in the woods until it was written the way they wanted.

This exasperated both me and her.

She wanted to reread it. And I couldn't allow her to. We were both under pressure. She was driven to despair. I thought I understood; but only afterwards, in prison, did I begin to really understand.

I'm someone who never had to lie a lot, before. As a transporter you're almost always silent. And even later, with my crime, I had little to do with the arrangements. It's in planning that you have to lie. Maybe you're at a bar with a close buddy, somebody you've worked with, served time in prison with, taken vacations with; maybe your families spend time together. And you already know that they've decided to kill him. And you can't tell him. And maybe you're the one who will have to do it.

I was spared all that.

During the kidnapping, rather than lying I made things up every now and then. And she knew it, it was practically agreed upon.

At home, when I was little, they always firmly insisted on being truthful.

They could forgive anything, but not a lie. Even repeating things that were true but that you didn't fully agree with was considered dishonest. You'll feel better, my mother said, if the words are in tune with you.

In prison I never signed false accusations. Or even true ones.

Maybe outside it's easier to lie. You say a thing that you don't agree with, and then you think about something else. You have so many choices. You're out and about. Not here. Here you're alone, with that voice that isn't yours. You have nothing else, and at some point you don't even recognize your own voice.

They said that photographing a hostage in a bra, if she's young, is useless, because somehow everyone takes it for granted that you're fucking her. Old ladies, instead, were photographed half-naked. A filthy cot, tangled hair, and them in a bra. So everyone would know that they were being mistreated, that they were dying day by day. Then they sent the photos to the newspapers. A rich old lady in a bra makes an impression on people. A rich old lady who is humiliated makes an impression on people. The newspapers didn't publish the photos, because back then there was still respect for the rich. But the pictures got around anyway. And often the family decided to pay. They realized that they had to get her out of there, right away, at any cost, before the photographs robbed the old woman of whatever life remained to her and traveled around the world in her place.

I photographed the Coffee Princess clothed.

Once we had to redo it, because she'd smiled slightly.

Not that she was happy. I delude myself about a lot of things but I don't really believe she was happy. It's just that in front of the camera she smiled, instinctively. You learn to smile at the camera from the time you are a child, and she smiled.

Photographs in a kidnapping serve to communicate two things: I'm still alive, therefore it makes sense to pay; and: Things are bad, do it quickly.

On this second point the Coffee Princess and I were a flop. Her expression might be grim or angry but never desperate. It was the face of someone who feels betrayed, abandoned by her family, like a child forgotten at school . . . But determined to make you pay for it.

Maybe I should have photographed her while she was writing the letters. When she no longer knew who she was, and became disconsolate. But I didn't think of it.

She was always asking me if they had published the photo, how she had come out.

The Coffee Princess cared about how she looked. I'm grateful to her for that. For all the times I later looked at those newspaper clippings and actually found a little beauty in them, in spite of everything.

They arrested me for that. But it would have happened anyway, only a little later on.

During the kidnapping, the newspapers they gave me were already censored, with nothing about the abduction. They didn't trust me. In prison too, they brought me the papers with things that had been cut out. There's always been this idea that there are things I shouldn't know.

All hostages want to read. Anything. They read a newspaper from top to bottom, even the ads. They savor it, like someone who only has one tea bag and reuses it forever, until he's only drinking hot water.

She even pored over years-old newspapers that were meant for other purposes . . . And she read some of the articles out loud. Then I started looking at the paper too, to try and see what she found in them. She preferred newspapers to magazines, magazines to books. It's normal. At the beginning of a period of captivity, the more recent a thing is, the more important it seems to you. That's why, on the tiers, there are those who prefer newscasts to movies: they figure they no longer need fantasy. They think that what happens outside is already extraordinary, incredible as it is, just because it's outside.

As for me, what I had to read I read on the island, before I killed. I read even at night, lying next to the fortified cell door to take advantage of the chink of light from the corridor. There were never enough hours. I had little time. I was in prison but I had little time. I read and reread some books so often that even now, if I had a normal memory, I'd be able to recite them inside my head. With my eyes closed.

The reason the newspapers for the Coffee King's daughter were given to me full of holes is because it's important that hostages remain in the dark. It's the best way to keep them calm. Their world must begin and end where the hideout begins and ends. The world is what we tell them.

It's like the interrogations: there are things about yourself that you would only tell God. And to become a god, those who interrogate you must keep you ignorant.

I was never fully convinced about that. I mean, for interrogations, sure. But we weren't interrogating the

Princess, what harm was there in letting her see one of her published photos?

I couldn't do much about it, though, because the newspapers they brought me were already clipped, and they weren't recent. Once they gave me a paper from that same day, with a huge section cut out. We had taken her photos the week before. All things considered, I realized that there must have been a photo there. Our photo. My snapshot and her face.

So I did something that could cost me my life: instead of going back to the hideout, I went into town, a two-hour walk, and bought the paper intact.

I also bought a toothbrush. Being without a toothbrush was torture for her. They didn't want to give her one, thinking: In a moment of despair, she'll stick it down her throat. But I knew she wasn't desperate. She wasn't happy, but she wasn't desperate either. Besides, it's not every day you see someone stick a toothbrush down his throat. When I kept asking them to bring a toothbrush they said: Does it disgust you to kiss her like that? Since then I hadn't asked for it again.

That day, however, I bought a newspaper that wasn't cut up, a toothbrush, clean underwear, a comb and two pizzas. Madness. In a small town, where everyone knows everybody. Fortunately, that wasn't a kidnapping zone. They watched me until I got on the bus, then they forgot about me. I got off two towns later, walked a long time, and once in the woods I opened the newspaper. There were two photos. One of her in her twenties, before she got married, had kids, and was kidnapped. And the photo that I took of her. She looked younger in my photograph, without makeup or earrings. The Coffee Princess was full of life, genuine and generous, even at twenty. But she'd had her hair done then. So I kept the photo of her as a captive, and I buried the twenty-year-old with the newspaper.

It was almost night when I got back to the hideout; the pizzas were cold of course, and she was inconsolable.

She had vomited on herself out of fear. She told me: I was afraid I'd die alone, in this hellhole, without food or water. She was sobbing. She couldn't stop. She told me: I thought, they've killed him, and I'll die here, alone, chained up. She told me she'd sooner I killed her, me, or another member of the band, rather than be left to die there, shackled, forgotten.

Me. Or another member of the band. I took it badly. By me or by someone else wasn't the same thing. Then I realized that maybe she was saying those unkind words to punish me for leaving her alone, and I forgave her. I showed her the photo. I gave her the toothbrush, the underwear, the comb, and we ate the pizzas. The toothbrush was enough to suddenly make her happy again. That's right, really happy. Prisoners go crazy over gifts. In prison I saw revolts quelled by distributing candy. I swear: candy. As a prisoner, you have the mood swings of a child, so that anything, even the smallest thing, is all you can focus on.

The name of the town and the address of the pizzeria were on the cardboard boxes. It was dark. We ate by candlelight, the olive-green tarp raised and held open with rocks. She didn't seem to have noticed the names. I took the boxes and threw them into the ravine, farther down than usual.

I'm glad I didn't kill her because of those two stupid boxes. It was my fault, I hadn't paid attention.

I kept the photo with me, even though it was like having stolen stuff on you. After the arrest I tried to get them to return it to me, but there was no way. I finally asked my lawyer to get a copy of the newspapers from that time and cut it out again. They burned it on me when I killed the guard. Now I've let it go. I know people who hang the victim's photo beside their pillow and talk to it every morning and every night. It's the last thing they see, before dark. The first thing, when it gets light.

Not me. I don't idealize her.

People locked up in a bare cell tend to fall in love easily, talk like a kid, dream like an adolescent, get emotional over music that's sickening. Not me.

They write letters to wives they've killed, to children they haven't raised. The concrete walls reflect it, unwilling to absorb all that sighing, those ill-timed emotions.

Only the first night when Piscio came to, and shouted nonstop until morning, only then was the concrete unable to avoid it.

After the time with the pizzas I decided that I would never leave her alone and chained again.

The following week, before going to the stable, I took off her chain and said: I'll be back by evening. But if I don't come back, continue to wait for me that night, the following day, and the night after that. If you haven't seen anyone by the morning of the second day, then go.

She was disoriented.

You're not handcuffing me? You're not putting my hood on either?

If I handcuff you and put your hood on it's as if I were keeping you chained. You'd fall into the ravine, you'd die there. I could gag you, that I could do. But I don't like the idea.

I reminded her that there was a second guard down below, in the woods. The bad guy. And if she tried to yell, or leave the hideout before the second day, he would shoot her callously, because he didn't like this job anymore, and he couldn't wait to go home.

The story about a bad guard is used all the time.

With her, after the early days, I didn't bother.

Even now I was skeptical about resorting to it. Captives like knowing that there is a bad kidnapper, that the malevolence is coming from a precise point. The good kidnapper unfortunately can't do anything about it, they are victims together.

She said: Thank you, and massaged her ankle.

I told her: Wait at least an hour, then look out if you want, but don't leave the hideout for any reason.

And I set off, with my backpack, like on any other contact day. I made a wide circuit, and from above, from behind a rock, I settled down to watch.

I had binoculars in the backpack but they didn't help much because the woods were too dense. To see the cave you had to be close by. That was another reason they had chosen the place.

Thinking back, the Princess and I could have used the binoculars to observe the stars. Spent some evenings like that.

Anyway, I was staring at the mouth of the cave, and after half an hour she came out. She didn't have a watch, she couldn't know that it hadn't yet been an hour. She gazed down into the ravine for a long time. At the plastic bags we threw away. The ferns and nettles. Then she went back inside and didn't come out again.

I stayed behind the rock all day to keep watch. Toward evening I too went back.

And there were never any problems.

The chain was only used when I was there with her.

Because when I was there, my gun was also there, in a corner of the hideout. She could have taken it. There was a map of the area besides. And the flashlight, for walking at night. It would have been a constant temptation. More importantly, she felt more optimistic, more spirited and stronger, when I was there with her. When I went away, however, everything, all the vitality went away with me. And she was left alone. The only thing she wanted was for me to come back quickly. The chains were no longer needed. She too only felt really safe in there. In that crappy hole. With me. In that grotto. There are no miracles without grottoes, with no earth and rocks around.

When it was windy we watched the trees. It always makes an impression because every branch moves on its own, and it doesn't seem possible that it's the same wind making them all move; you get the feeling that it's them, tormented, tossing about.

Before I released her, I had to teach her to walk again.

We went outside every day, for an hour, to exercise. They had ordered me to. Her muscles were atrophying and she had to be able to walk the trail leading to the road.

To walk. I'm the one who brings you food, clothing, water to drink and wash yourself. It's right that I should be the one to teach you to walk.

To walk away from me.

That hurt me a little. A crack in my heart that widened.

They were all exercises done in place, because the ravine's drop began right outside the shelter. But at least we could stand up. She clung to me, and it wasn't the first time.

Hostages cling a lot, because often they can't see. They're blindfolded, and you have to guide them over debris, wet grass, pebbly stream banks.

Sometimes they grip you so tight it cuts off your circulation. Because they're scared.

On the first day of the kidnapping, as soon as we reached the hideout, we left her alone for a while. She was tired and the narcotic still hadn't worn off. After a few hours I looked in and, absurdly, she asked me: Who are you?

I'm the one who took your hand in the woods, I told her.

I thought you made me get out to kill me.

No, it was just the end of the road.

Months later she told me that the smell of my jacket was the one thing that had remained stamped in her memory that first day. In her mind she called me Buffalo, because I'd seemed big while she was blindfolded, and more gentle than the others, and because I smelled of leather; she hoped I would always be there.

They make up lots of names during kidnappings.

They all do it: male and female, young and old. Some of them are spirited and some lose heart. Often the names are those of animals. Names from fairy tales. Because suddenly everything has changed. Being held captive is like a spell. And you don't know when food or punishment is coming. Beauty is held prisoner by the beasts, and doesn't know how many there are; they say little, and are almost always distant.

When they decided to leave only me in the hideout to watch her, she stopped calling me Buffalo, and I stopped calling her Princess. Names are useful to evoke

those who aren't there. We were always there. We had
no need to distinguish ourselves from anyone else: if it
wasn't me, it was her. In those few square feet if we
wanted to talk, we just had to start. At night, we just had
to whisper: Are you awake? It's easier to talk in the dark.
You pay more attention, you seem to understand better.

The Princess clung to me on the last day as well.

We went to those woods in the spring, we left there
in the fall. We missed one season. That's why, in a sense,
we were limping anyway, in spite of the exercises.
Because it was not an entire full year.

From time to time she leaned her head on my shoulder. This was something she hadn't done during the earlier trek. At the time, I deluded myself into thinking
that it was something more than fear, more than the
rugged trail, the stream down in the ravine, and the
brush that scratched her legs. The delusion that she
wanted to hold me back.

Then I saw her on television, six hours later, and I
realized that I meant nothing. That for her, I ended
where the woods ended. Gone, along with the cold.

On the news she was radiant, like most of those who
are released. Radiant from fear that is transformed into
elation. It's their celebration. Baptism and wedding
together. Police cars with horns blaring. Photographers,
TV cameras. Strangers cheering and weeping for joy. The
whole neighborhood welcoming them like one of their
own. People who didn't know you now stop you on the
street, call you by name, hug you. That's how people are.
When someone is held captive in a place, even for only

a couple of months, it strikes their imagination. Especially the poor. Some poor people cry if they know that a wealthy person is forced to lead a terrible life for a couple of months, because they know he isn't used to it. They cry for princesses. They cry because they think it's important for someone to live well from start to finish.

All kidnapped women are princesses. Anyone who messes with fairy tales is looking for trouble.

The police clean up the kidnapped victims before they put them on display before the TV cameras. There is always a bathtub ready, at police stations.

For a while, the victims are grateful to everyone they meet. The world is new, only just recreated, expressly for them. And at the same time it's the same as it always was, reassuring, recovered a moment before being forgotten. They are thirty-year-old newborns. You see them on TV and you feel like kidnapping them all over again. You change your mind. You think: I should have cut you up into little pieces, eaten you, fed you to the wild boars. Not let you go, and then see you so happy, so radiant at not seeing me anymore.

But you can think whatever you want, because by now she's a long distance away, and you have to keep hiding, alone. The worst part for you is just beginning. Whereas in her all that suppressed vitality explodes, propelling her far away. For a while she will feel freer. Freer than anyone who has never been held captive. Like someone who sets down a heavy suitcase, whose hands then feel weightless. She'll say: I learned things that matter, I shrugged off the rest. For a while, at least. Her hands free to hold other hands.

When we leave prison we are not so radiant.

Maybe because we stay locked up longer. Or maybe we don't experience the terror that kidnapped victims feel at the end: Are they moving me to free me, or to kill me?

They turned off the flow of drugs and decided to turn a blind eye on fermented fruit. Even buying a little extra therapy is now difficult. The prison has become filled with transparent plastic bags containing two or three liters of water, sugar, yeast and chunks of fruit. You see the purplish foam from the fermentation, you smell the putrid, sweetish odor in the corridors. As if the garbage piling up in the intermural area had risen up to the tiers. But drinking garbage makes you hostile. The drunks rob, fight, keep you awake. The more years you spend locked up, the harder it is to sleep. You're constantly wondering what time it is, like in a nursing home or any other place where time is the most important thing. Here they serve breakfast at 5 a.m., lunch at noon, supper at 5 p.m. Maybe those schedules are convenient for those who work the shifts, who knows, but they certainly make the night seem longer to us. On the tiers, where they are permitted to cook with camp stoves, they delude themselves into thinking they have a different life just because they can decide when to eat. But even if you eat at eight, your time zone is still that of the prison. And at nine you'll think about some therapy, like everyone else. By eleven you'd like to be sound asleep, but you can't sleep, and you're wishing for the therapy cart again, with its empty-tin-can sound. For the big shiny cart, jolting along, empty and light, making the air vibrate. Like a white galleon. It's as big as the food cart but all it contains are little tinkling bottles that help you to sleep. It rolls along on untiled floors: concrete coated with a glossy paint, washable, slippery when wet. A brownish color, like down here, or dark red, like on the tiers. There are black scrape marks left by the wheels of the food carts, by the black soles of the guards' boots, and by the white soles of sneakers which, though white, leave black scuff marks. Only the therapy cart doesn't leave any traces.

The enormous amount of therapy they used to bring Piscio . . .

We all stole it. Only those who have just entered don't understand. In the early months, in a place where you have no decisions to make, you can sleep as many as sixteen consecutive hours. But it's dangerous. Those who have a short sentence may think: I'm going to sleep through this. I'll sleep through it, and in three years I'll wake up a free man. But when others realize it, they begin to occupy the space that you no longer have the will, or the energy, to inhabit yourself. You risk waking up in the middle of the night, with a start, when it's already too late.

I too at the beginning thought: Finally I'll be able to get some sleep. Driving the van, with no obligatory rest stops, with no chrono-tachograph, you can go as many as thirty hours on end . . . When they arrested me I thought: All the sleep I missed while driving I'll make up for in the cell. I imagined it as a cabin: a small, quiet place, private, where you are by yourself. But you're never really alone, never really safe, in a cell. Not even down here. And even when you're alone, it's never quiet.

After a kidnapping it's normal to wonder: Will we meet again? Will you want to see me, when you're not forced to? Can two people really be so close, round the clock, for weeks, months, sometimes years . . . And then, abruptly, not see each other again?

Many kidnappers phone after the kidnapping is over, and nearly all the victims respond, go to meet them. Male or female, it makes no difference. Newspapers don't write about it but the police know it: when they aren't able to make an arrest right away, they begin tailing the victim. If they catch the two, the victim will say that she only accepted out of fear.

I figured on waiting a year and then calling. There wasn't time: they stopped me three months later, on the highway. With the van full of counterfeit goods. Because a kidnapping isn't enough for you to stop working, particularly if it isn't you who organizes it.

You think about arrest a lot, at first. You wonder: How will it happen? Will I be aware of them, will I hear them coming? Thinking about arrest is a little like thinking about death. I've always thought about death, it's a family trait: my grandmother thought about it from the time she was a girl, and my father as well. You try to imagine it, hoping that when the time comes it will be less frightening. Will I see the signs around me? Will I have time to prepare?

The customs officers, taking me away, said: Don't worry, you have a clean record, we're interested in whoever hired you to transport the stuff . . . But I knew that for me that date was equivalent to a milestone birthday. What I mean is, there are those who get arrested so often that they can't remember, but for me it was an Arrest with a capital A. The one that brings your life to a grinding halt. The van stopped in the turnout. That's what I remember: a van, practically new, with a trunk full of goods to be delivered, shaken by blasts of air raised by other trucks as they sped by, and all those shoes and handbags, fake but beautiful, concealed in there. In the dark.

On the way to the station people usually look at girls, bicycles, the mountains. Shop windows. Janitors sweeping in front of buildings. Normal things that suddenly seem exceptional. But I was on the highway. So I looked at the van. And then at the names of the cities painted in white on the pavement and on signs overhead, at the interchanges. And right away I saw those names as meaningless, without a city behind them, false. I wondered: How long will it be, how long, before I can choose where to turn off again?

At the station I stared down at my hands. Commander once told me: By now they could record your pupils with a beam of light and store the result on computers. But they'd rather stain you, press your fingers into the ink pad. It's useless for you to rub at it, wash it, you'll only dirty the soap. You have to wait for your skin to absorb it. After a few days the stain enters your blood, and externally you can't see it. And as I stared at my hands, the sergeant who was doing an inventory of my wallet found the photograph of the Princess. Someone else might have written 'newspaper clipping' and passed over it, but I had to get a cop who looked up and asked: Why do you carry this? Then he informed his captain. The captain, to avoid any hassles, sent a report to the chief investigator. And the chief investigator, who apparently no longer knew which way to turn, came to see me.

The next time he came, he also brought the Princess.

She listened to me, watching from behind a dark glass. And she recognized me. There was no way she couldn't. I think I would have felt badly if she hadn't. The recognition couldn't be admitted in a trial, but the chief investigator didn't care. He said to me: You're lucky, the first one caught can take his pick. You were simply a guard, and you treated the hostage humanely. If you cooperate, you'll do three years' time and we'll put you to work outside. Take us to the hideout. Give us names.

But I didn't talk.

Look, we'll catch them anyway in the course of a year, the chief said, and the others will talk, you'll see. Then you won't have anything left to sell. Show us where the weapons are.

I didn't talk.

Where's the money?

Then the chief sent me to the island, in a helicopter. The island was like a huge interrogation room. But I kept my mouth shut.

There was a guy on the island who talked in his sleep. At some point the guards became aware of it and began recording him, until something that could be used in the trials slipped out.

When they told him about it, he slit his throat. That was the climate there. Even if you talked in your sleep, you were still an informer. It's only right that you die. As long as your words are worth something, you have to remain silent.

Now it's different. Informers are considered odious individuals, true, but they're also seen as shrewd. People who know how to look out for number one. Individuals worthy of respect. Guys you can sit with at a bar.

Having been locked up for twenty years, I inspire great respect as far as words go. But deep down they consider me an old asshole.

Yet I would do it all again.

Individuals who turned traitor regretted it, even those who avoided the punishment they deserved. They regretted it because the moment comes, when they escort you before the judge, when you see that the cops are suddenly gentle with you, that they shake your hand and tell you how courageous you were, that your act will save lives. The words are sincere, because they always assign some young idiots to escort the informers, the first times . . . Then in front of the judge, however, they talk about money. Time and money. Which is the same thing. And the judge looks at you for what you are: a man who let himself be bought. And the young idiot who escorts you back to the cell tells you he'll pray for you, and if everyone did what you did . . . And then you realize you lost. You realize that you're a trained animal. That before you were a pariah, but now you've become the pariah of pariahs. Your tattoos, which earlier meant something, are suddenly just doodles. You betrayed a family where someone was constantly plotting to kill someone, where you lived in fear of being the next target, but at least they recognized you. They called you by name to make you turn around, to shoot you, in the street, but they called you by name. Now, after a few months of interrogation, you are entitled to a false name. To having the tattoos erased with a laser.

Because ultimately, that's what tattoos are for: to ensure that you won't turn traitor.

Only the N's still get tattoos. On their faces, on their eyes, on their fingers, as if to say: I'll never be able to hide them.

Our local criminals know that if you talk, the police aren't bothered by tattoos.

Tattoos, certain tattoos, only cause problems for an individual who wants to change his life without becoming an informer, and has to look for a job, pick the kids up at school. And then maybe, one night when he's drunker and more desperate than usual, he'll rinse his face with acid. And he'll be screwed just the same, because who will ever hire a person with acid-scarred skin.

The only tattoo I have is a coffee bean, on my right wrist.

I've always been appalled by the things used in prison to make ink, appalled by the makeshift needles.

The N's still decapitate snitches. But they have a problem that we no longer face: they're young. They suffer more being alone.

On the island I stopped eating for weeks, until they were forced to take me to the infirmary, where the doctor asked me 'What happened?' And finally I could talk.

Or else I waited for the interrogators, even though I knew what they would do to me, and that I wouldn't answer, but still I would hear their voices.

Even talking to Piscio, I even went that far . . . You have to have someone, your head can't stay mute.

Piscio was called that because he peed his pants. They said his wiener wept because of the things he'd done. But the truth is that a lot of people here suffer from incontinence. The muscles of men who for years live no more than a couple of feet from a toilet, with nothing better to do than listen to their urges, day and night . . . they get out of the habit. It's inevitable. Then during the transfers you pay for it. The difference is that Piscio didn't hold it in even in the cell. And he wasn't capable of demanding that the infirmary provide the diapers he was entitled to, or keeping them from being stolen from him when they did bring them. He never washed. He wasn't able to do anything. Being in the same corridor with Piscio was torture for everyone: guards as well as inmates.

And so we tormented him.

It's hard to feel compassion for someone like that. I only managed to do so the first two nights of the week when he yelled non-stop. For me at least, what he'd done outside had nothing to do with it. I didn't care about that. Here the more the new guys—young men free until a short time ago—vie for power, the greater the contempt they have for pedophiles. I believe it's because every now and then you feel the need to be on the side of what's indisputably right. Even an informer can think he's better than Piscio. That's why they stuck broomsticks up his rear end, why we threw bars of soap at him on the way to the shower. Anyone can talk to a pedophile, he's not allowed to talk to anybody. Anyway Piscio was revolting, pedophile or not.

He had diabetes. And because we used to take away his insulin, by now he was almost blind. And because one of the many things we did was to systematically break his glasses, he really couldn't see anything anymore. He spent his time in his cell like a pink mole, encrusted, protected only by filth.

Commander, like me, also thought it was wrong. But Commander, like me, couldn't help doing it.

The only time Piscio saw anything and was clean, and occasionally understood, was when he came off the medication, once a month. For three days prior to that, the guards and the nurse would check to make sure he took all his meds, in front of them. Shortly before he came out of it, they showed up to wash him down with hoses. Then they dressed him. They put on the glasses they kept just for those occasions, because when he came to, it was essential that he see. The doctors showed him photographs and drawings. Even videos. And they measured his reactions. A guard escorted him, citing security as an excuse. The truth is that it was free porn. And more importantly, the guard could tell about it afterwards and laugh along with the entire prison. They showed Piscio nude women and children in a swimming pool. Pictures of cherubic tots and naked ladies.

Kids playing and adults wrestling. Children biting into fruit. Naked children. Sex between consenting adults. In black and white or in color.

Piscio got aroused indiscriminately. Everyone gets aroused somewhat indiscriminately in here, or they don't get aroused at all anymore.

Then they brought him back down, took away his glasses and started dropping soap bars again. With the excuse that he was a suicide risk, he had to remain naked in the cell. With not a stitch. The truth is that he wasn't at risk, at least at the time, but the guards like bare places: easier to check. And to clean. So that Piscio, even if he could see and had the reflexes to cover himself, had no defenses whatsoever. He had to let them whack him. He whined, every now and then, but he took it. He only hid his face with his hands whenever anyone passed, including volunteers. Because back then there were still volunteers, and they roamed around the prison. They didn't interact with Piscio: he was too blind, filthy, incoherent. But they wrote to Commander. They started talking about it outside. It was their way of reacting to the disgust, the stench that assailed them when they passed through there. Until Commander decided that enough was enough: he couldn't take the chance. From that time on, Piscio would take his medicines every day, under the strict supervision of the guards. If you stole something of his you'd be looking for trouble. And if you threw your soap at him, you wouldn't get it back, you'd have to do without. And that's when the tragedy occurred. All because of those volunteers, in the end. Because after a month of taking his meds, Piscio began to realize a thing or two. He didn't understand much, but some things certainly. They left the glasses he used for medical visits in his cell. And they kept him clean, always, so that the volunteers started going to see him. He asked questions and they made inquiries, then responded. As a result, he discovered that he had been locked up for seventeen years, and that his mother had continued writing to him for nine years but he hadn't been aware of it. She had even come to see him but he had not gone to the visitation room. He hadn't understood, or they hadn't told him. No word of her, afterwards, for eight years. So the volunteers made more inquiries, and Piscio found out that she had died. The first night he yelled not because she was dead but because he hadn't known about it. That night, and the next, we felt compassion for him. Both us and the guards, for the first time. There was something horrific, irremediable in those screams. And when he yelled that he wanted to die, we were quick to tell him no, not now that you're beginning to live again . . .

Starting the third night we began telling him: Do it. Kill yourself. Do it right now and stop blubbering. Let us get some sleep.

They took away his glasses to avoid any trouble.

People now wait for the guard to be at the end of the corridor before they hang themselves, or for their neighboring cell mates to be almost awake before they kick over the stool. The guard comes running, wraps his arms around the man, saves him. He lifts the body, so the man won't strangle, holds it tight, while the inmates shout, bang on the cell bars, to call for help.

There are people willing to do anything, even let themselves be embraced. But when the would-be suicide comes back from the infirmary, the ribbing begins. Welcome back. You saved my life! Don't ever try it again!

But no one has saved anything. There is no life, there's nothing. There's no serious intent.

Someone who really wants to hang himself puts on a wet bathrobe, to weigh more. Soaps up the sheets so they'll slide more easily. Then binds his hands to resist the temptation to free himself at the last moment. Above all, he waits until there's really no one around. There's always a time, even in the most crowded cell, there's always a moment when no one can save you. If you'd rather use a razor-blade, you soak it in water and garlic, so the wound won't heal. You'll aim for the jugular, if you are serious and don't have much time, not the wrists. You'll keep your legs elevated, so the blood will flow out more quickly. If you choose a cut that takes more than half an hour for you to bleed to death, it's because you don't really want to die.

Piscio was kept naked, without glasses, with no razor-blades and no sheets. Yet he succeeded in killing himself just the same, ripping his veins open with his teeth.

It's the only thing for which he deserves a little respect.

Now people cut themselves and they save them, they cut themselves and they save them, until the skin is so marked with scars, on their arms, shoulders, chest, that they look like zebras. Stupid animals held captive in a zoo.

They cut themselves, they hang themselves . . . botching it each time.

If you're a guard it's different. They have an advantage there too. They go to the armory, get a gun, and it's over.

It's cold.

I felt cold last night, then all day long today, and now that it's dark again, I feel even colder.

The guard on the outer wall is rain-soaked. His vest is as old as the prison: armor plates and cotton pockets; it doesn't do any good and, in the rain, weighs even more. But no one cares, because they put the burn-outs on the perimeter wall, those who no longer have the strength to fight, to listen to lies, to tell them. They station them there, up top, with binoculars and an automatic rifle. Once it was almost considered a reward: a chair, a heater, a radio, newspapers. Now, however, if a guard stays cozy inside the watchtower, he gets a written warning, and if he keeps it up, they suspend him without pay. These are things that we aren't supposed to know: the guards' fantasy is to know all about us, without us knowing anything about them, but that's impossible in such close circumstances. You hear them talking, complaining. The long shifts, no vacation, overtime in arrears ... From the control room they phone those who are on sick leave, threatening, begging, every day, but those guys get the doctor to write that they're depressed. And most of the time it's not even a lie, because looking down at an empty yard, in the rain, is depressing.

Today only the N's went outside.

Running in a fine drizzle takes discipline, only addicts run in a downpour. The N's run even when the only sound is that of their soles on the wet pavement, and the clamor of those who stayed indoors in the game room, doing who knows what. Today it's raining on all the prisons of the world. Packs of superfluous males, crowded together and left to rot. Even more closed in on a rainy Sunday: the sliding bars, the heavy cell doors, the inner wall, the outer wall, and then the rain besides. Bars of rain that you can't break through, that make a racket when they smack the ground. Sunday's bars that prevent mail delivery, trips to trials or hospitals. No documents to discuss with the records office. Some have visitors, others wait for evening, the same for everyone. No more fresh air until tomorrow.

So they drink, on the tiers and in the barracks. They watch television.

If the guards have just come back from vacation, they uncork liqueurs from their home towns, they become sentimental and don't bother anyone. But when their vacations are canceled, they buy cheap bottles at the guards' commissary and guzzle them at room temperature, even if they should be cold. They drink whether or not they are on duty. Young college grads and older men with a secondary school diploma; guys who signed up already drunk, by mistake, forty years ago.

The inmates have to make do with fermented fruit and television. On television it isn't raining. There are offices full of light, and African animals. On television it's hot. Everyone tries to get into the act, grab their share. And when there's a big disaster it's even better because they think: What's happening is so incredibly important that even those outside must be watching it, everyone, no one excluded. They won't be playing with their kids, they won't be making out, they won't be going to the shore or working to make money. It makes you feel you're in the right place, watching live. Watching from a cell counts as much as watching from a living room.

On the island, following the relief efforts for an earthquake on television, the prisoners decided to take up a collection. They, the more fortunate ones, wanted to give something to those who no longer had anything, not even a prison roof to shelter them from the rain. For once they were the more fortunate . . . It was exhilarating. Commander did not okay it. He said that the weaker detainees would feel obligated to participate, they would go into debt, and debts lead to knifings. Which would create a security problem.

Obviously it wasn't true. It was just that, as he saw it, nothing should come from a prison, as though it were a black hole. The fact is that the collection didn't happen. And after a few days, only the inmates and the guards, and some old person at home, some loser, were left watching the news about the earthquake. Increasingly brief reports, at increasingly odd hours.

Some nights on the island the guards would leave the television on and go out to fire rounds, because they realized that we—us and them—were absurdly watching the exact same programs. In the cell or in the barracks, the same zebra was being shown, killed at the same moment, by the same lion ... For us and for them, all of us equal, and for no one else but us, because those outside who were free had already stopped watching hours ago.

The guards kept firing until their arms went numb, then the singing started, along with the body searches and rattling the bars.

The same singing these guys are doing now. Here they can't shoot, but when they're drunk, staggering and clinging to one another, they always sing the same songs. Among the thousand possible insults, always the same words. They hurl the empty bottles against the walls and bang on the bars. It had been years since they made such a racket, clanging the keys loudly against the metal. Until last year they would have moved the curtain aside with one hand and then knocked quietly, practically apologizing. It annoyed us: Were they afraid of ruining the paint? The prison was always freshly painted, until last year. There were times when the guards didn't even seem like guards anymore; then we weren't sure what we were, and started resenting them. Couldn't they even bang properly? Bang like they're doing now, so they could tell from the sound whether the bars were still solid or whether someone surreptitiously cut them and left them there for appearances, ready to allow someone to escape.

If you wrap a fuel cylinder in a rag soaked in oil and set fire to it, the heat puts the gas under pressure and the canister explodes. It doesn't do a lot of damage, but it does make noise; it's disorienting, it resounds. With a bit of luck, it can burst the eardrums. Or you can puncture the canister and use it as a welder's torch. Or just bring the oil to a boil and throw it. If you mix it with jam before throwing it, it will become stickier, and the burns will be more severe. A toothbrush handle heated on a camp stove, then hardened in cold water and scraped on rough concrete becomes a spike. When the prison sharpens its weapons, you hear a hum like the whirring of cicadas, as though summer has come. And the mood is like that too: that of a new season. Newspapers vanish. There is a way of rolling them up that makes them harder than wood. The printed words don't matter anymore. You don't notice the pages, you have a weapon in your hands. And those who don't use the papers to make clubs put them under their shirts to cushion knife blows.

A bar of soap in a sock becomes a sling that can crack a temple. The prison is full of innocent things that can kill, and they've left them all to us.

Newspaper, soap and a toothbrush can kill.

How come they seized the mosquito nets and left the gas canisters?

Wherever they see something white, the guards soil it. They trampled on the toothpaste. Now there's mud on the floor. They squeezed out the tubes and stomped on them with their boots. The toothpaste that in commercials ends up on the teeth of women and children.

They removed the cardboard cores from the rolls of toilet paper.

They confiscated thermoses, because of the double bottom. They appropriated any padded, quilted or lined jackets. Only one woolen hat is permitted, with no flaps. Turtleneck sweaters and hooded sweatshirts are prohibited: the face must be clearly visible, even from above, or from a distance.

Pants with metal buttons are prohibited. Watches are prohibited. Only a single pair of gloves is permitted.

They took little from me, because I've always had little. In solitary, whatever you have must fit into a single cardboard carton: you have to choose, there's no room for anything useless. On the tiers, on the other hand, there were no limits until tonight. People with overflowing lockers, like some old people's homes, with boxes on top of the locker, under the bed, beside the sink. The guys up there are constantly asking for things from family members, lawyers, visiting clergymen, in person or by letter. Their heads are so filled with the things they want that then on visiting day they can't even hear what's said, the sounds come through muffled, as if they had a cold. And they feel like leaping at the throat of the idiot who came to see them, who three hours earlier was outside and will soon be out there again, in a world with an abundance of things, and all he's brought them is three or four . . . not even the right ones.

But starting tonight even up on the floors they'll have to learn to fit everything into three cartons. The guards threw all the rest of it in the corridors and the attendants will haul it away. Photos of thighs, and trial documents that aren't supposed to be seized, but they take them anyway. All the hearings, testimonies and convictions, mixed together. They even smashed the shelves made from cigarette packets, because the walls must remain bare for inspection, in accordance with the regulations. For years they hadn't taken them down. That's the purpose of searches, to remind you that what you have, what you've acquired, assembled, what you feel is yours is here today and gone tomorrow.

Meanwhile, the glaring lights in the intermural zone attract mosquitoes from over the mountains. They even come from the sea. The weaker lights draw them into the cells. They smell our blood, our odor, the fact that we can't get away. By morning you find yourself swollen, disfigured, with no rest and no blood. The insects that crawl out of the walls, from holes you can hope to plug with toothpaste, are one thing; the ones that come from outside, from the air beyond the windows, are another story. If only Commander would come down again, I would get on my knees and beg him, in the name of all the years we've spent together: Give us back the mosquito nets before summer.

The porters are so worn out they can't feel their arms anymore, but they don't pay any attention because the only thing that matters now is to talk about the boy.

That is, it matters to those on the third tier, which is Toro's floor, and on the first, where the N's are. For everyone else, the problem is how to keep from going insane now that they've seized the few remaining drugs, and it will be days before the fruit ferments again, and there are still sixteen hours to go before the therapy cart comes around, and all that's left is the gas from the camp stoves to hope for sleep.

But to Toro and to the N's it matters, and how.

The N's are wondering how much Toro is still willing to put up with, what the guards can do to him and still get away with. It seems that during the search a guard slashed the boy's mattress and found an envelope. And in the envelope there were letters and photos. When the drunken guard took a photo and began licking it, the boy jumped him.

Toro separated them, but by then the damage was done.

They'll beat the boy up for sure tonight, in the few hours that remain.

They could put it off, but they'll do it right away, to prove they don't need to dodge it. If they haven't sent him down here, to isolation, it's because they want to beat him up on the tiers. Where Toro can see. Where the N's can hear.

You would expect that a photo hidden in the mattress would at least show the girl naked, but instead she was in a swimsuit. Everyone says so. The boy will let them beat him up over a photo in a swimsuit, taken in prison. The place is full of photos taken inside to be looked at and kept inside. Photos that have nothing to do with the outside world. They're usually taken in groups, in the yard, like class photos to remember who was with you. But there are also photos for lovers, like this one, sent from one prison to another. At one time you stood in front of a section of wall with a poster of a forest, or a picture of the sea; now though the backgrounds are added later, on the computer. A person sits on a bucket, and later it becomes a motorcycle. They transform the prison yard into whatever you want: palaces, oceans, mountains. You just have to pay. The prison photographer's job is much sought-after. It allows you to move about, earn some money, keep a camera and a computer. They usually assign it to informers. In the big prisons, where there are many informers, and two or three photographers, clients choose them based on the backgrounds they have to offer you, like a hundred years ago. The boy's girlfriend chose a bathing establishment, not the usual white, deserted, unending tropical beaches that everyone wants. She chose a nearby location, for families, easy to get to and inexpensive.

You can tell she's a sober girl. You can see that's what she has in mind for the day she gets out.

She had herself photographed in a one-piece suit, the kind that aren't worn much anymore. A bathing suit from fifty years ago, a modesty from fifty years ago. She has a radiant gaze and it's directed at only one person, in another prison: the boy.

They're beautiful together.

Too bad their sentences are out of phase, and will be even more so after tonight.

Since the boy fell in love he stopped hanging women's photos on the wall. He started drawing. For more than a year he's been drawing buffalos and forests, huge full moons, wolves, waterfalls, horses, camp fires. All things he's never seen, and which tonight were seized from him. Toro's cell mate avoided getting any disciplinary notes after he fell in love, because every sentence reduction became important, so she would have less time to wait for him. But after tonight he'll get out even later, long after her.

If I know Commander, when they brought him that half-torn photo, he must have had a moment of suspicion. Why hide it in the mattress, why go so far as to attack a guard? Is there something I'm not getting, some trafficking that I'm missing, some secret code?

That's one of the curses of prison. Never being able to trust anyone.

Always asking yourself not: What is it?, but: What is it hiding?

Especially the guards. The less trusting they are, the more adept they become. But trust is an inevitable secretion, and keeping it inside hurts after a while.

I bet Commander showed the photograph to a criminal symbols specialist. A girl in a black, one-piece bathing suit, sitting on a paddle boat, does it mean anything? Why is she smiling? Why are there three umbrellas behind her? Why are her legs crossed, with her arms over her legs, as if she were naked, and instead she's wearing a one-piece bathing suit? Why is the bathing suit black, even though she's young and doesn't need to look slimmer?

Commander must have called the capital and spoken with a specialist, even though he was already certain of the answer.

And the criminal symbols specialist must have confirmed: She's just being modest.

At that point Commander, if I know him, would have closed his eyes and licked the photograph, filled with sadness. Because the boy lost control when the guard started licking it. Maybe symbols had nothing to do with it, or decency either. Maybe it was the usual drug mixed with the photo's ink. But I'm sure that Commander, when he licked it, must have only detected the taste of a photograph kept hidden too long in a mattress, and then licked, before him, by a drunken guard.

They require knee pads, a helmet for their heads, gloves for their hands; to cover their eyes, a visor. Foam rubber, leather, Kevlar. Over the chest, in front of the heart, bulletproof ceramic plates.

As if the boy might have a gun.

They're getting ready. Leg guards, arm guards. Clubs, shields, spray. We're born too fragile. Velcro that opens and closes, opens and closes again, to tighten better, remove air, eliminate any space between the armor and the skin. The guards' uniforms are blue, but the riot gear they wear for beatings is black. To vanish into blackness. There is no mimetic or institutional reason, it's not easier to wash, or more resistant. Black absorbs the fear of those who wear it and projects it outward.

The equipment room, in the basement of the guards' building, is like a ski rental shop: the back room where everyone is trying on ski boots, walking around awkwardly and getting help with the bindings when it's too difficult. Then they say: It's suffocating in here, I'm going to head out. Except no one can leave the equipment room without an order.

I can hear them.

I hear them scurrying like rats as they're about to go beat someone. The door closes again. I hear them walking, then speeding up to a trot, almost without being aware of it. Having to stay put, down here, I've become rooted in the cement, with nerves that can sense the entire prison. If someone walks in the corridor under the yard it's like he were walking on my left arm.

The only thing I can't sense is light.

But in Toro's cell it's just been turned off, I know. I imagine it.

There too they are getting ready, in their own way.

Toro must have tried to put together the bits of foam from the mattress the guards slashed, to put between the boy and the cot. To let him get a little rest, in the minutes or hours before being beaten.

He must have told him: When they come, jump out from under the blankets right away. Don't tuck them in. Go to sleep dressed, but don't overdo it, otherwise they'll get pissed and strip you naked. Go to sleep with your jumpsuit, with a light sweater underneath. If you need something, I'll lend it to you. Don't tuck the covers in: you have to be able to jump out of bed yourself, because if they do it, it's worse. Put this razor blade in your mouth, he must have told him, you have to sleep with it, because they charge in fast, and there's no time to reach for it at that moment. When they come, cut yourself right away. You have to move your tongue and hold the blood in your mouth. Your blood is the only thing they're afraid of. They're not afraid of you, but they are afraid of your germs. And they might also be afraid of having hurt you too badly, of having left too many lasting signs. On the island they beat you black and blue because they knew that the doctors were theirs, time was theirs. They could hang you in the cell, at worst, but even on the island they tried to avoid fractures and scars.

Fear of autopsies.

Fear of what the dead can tell in court.

Toro is probably explaining: It's important that they see the blood. You shouldn't spit it on them, otherwise they'll quickly bolt, and then you're done for. It takes attention to detail, even for bleeding. You have to make a glob, let it ooze out and then spread it around with your hands as you keep shielding yourself from the blows. And then, only when you have a good deal of blood on you, will you start screaming. Then I'll shout, too, Toro must have said. The whole tier will shout. And for a moment the shift from silence to shouting will make them stop. That's when you stop shielding yourself and let them see the blood. It's risky, but unavoidable. That's the only way they'll really calm down. They'll beat you a little longer and then they'll go. Watch out for unexpected blows. There's always someone who turns back to give you one last kick, the most severe. All in all, however, with a couple of days in the infirmary you should be okay. The important thing is for the guards not to feel like they've been tricked, for them to feel satisfied, so they can say: That'll teach him.

Such silence.

Only when something is about to happen is it really silent in a prison.

With silence like this nobody can sleep. All you can do is lie still, in bed, listening. The boy must be listening too, with the razor blade in his mouth. A steel pacifier that's nice and sharp. He's holding his breath. The whole tier is holding its breath. They're coming. Like a black locomotive. One hand gripping the shield, the other resting on the shoulder of the guard in front of him. The security gates open as they pass, along with the sally ports. Each tier is divided in two by a sally port with four gates: one to the east, one to the west, one for the stairs leading up, one for those that go down. In the sally port are the elevator, a desk and two chairs for the guards. The sally ports are the prison's intersections. However, their purpose is not to enable movement but to impede it. Like a knee that's always swollen. They prevent those on the east from going to the west, those below from going up. The sally ports are often empty, especially during the night shift, because there aren't enough guards to monitor them all. But tonight, faced with the black locomotive, the sally ports are all unlocked. The prison is wide open.

The guards climb the stairs, because the elevator is too small to hold them.

By the time they reach the floor, their neck protectors are soaked with sweat and they're panting in their helmets, but it doesn't matter: they're euphoric. They've forgotten Sunday, the dead prison.

They're the living prison, now, running.

Only fifty more yards.

In front of Toro's cell, the guard on duty opens the armored door and the bars, then squeezes against the wall to let them pass so he won't get trampled.

No more than two will actually be able to beat the boy, since the cell is as small as a broom closet. The others are only there to urge them on, to make the course set by the first two irreversible.

There's the sound of a stool.

Heaven help you if you try to protect yourself with a stool: with one blow of the club they'll knock it out of your fingers, with a kick they'll roll it out of reach, as far out of reach as you can in a cell. The stool has ended up against the pots, under the sink. That's the sound of pots. That instead is the sound of the guards furiously raising and lowering their clubs, raising and lowering their clubs, pistons of a black engine. They're relentless. Their visors are steamed over. Their breath is hot, the cell cold. They grunt.

Toro doesn't make a sound. He's listening. There are so many things you have to learn not to hear, in a small space. Not to hear those who are stroking themselves, the ones who are snoring, someone who is ill if you can't help him. Not to hear when they're beating someone is harder. To lie there unmoving, like Toro, as the cell rumbles, and your cot shakes, and you're demonstrating to the entire prison that you are unable to protect the boy, just as you once couldn't protect a son . . .

There, now's the time. He shouts. They shout. Shout!

The boy must have opened his arms, he must be showing them the blood.

They shout some more. They go on shouting. Why? Maybe the blood didn't stop them. They keep pounding away, punching into the blood; it feels good, like stomping their feet in a puddle. A systematic thrashing, finally, now that the boy has opened his arms, and the shell can no longer close up. He can crumple, that he can do, like a sheet of paper in a blaze. Not to protect himself, when there's nothing left to protect. Just the body that, left to itself, tends to occupy less space.

Now they call out, he needs help.

The guards must be gone, at last.

This time they really did some damage. Not an injury for the infirmary, a hospital case.

They return walking slowly. In the corridor under the yard they take off their helmets.

Some must be complaining about how difficult it is to wash away blood, because the special gear, unlike the uniforms, can't be sent to the prison laundry. And someone will say—because there's always someone who says it—that at one time he preferred to buy a vest with his own money, rather than go nuts rubbing away the stains . . . And someone else will chime in: Sure, give the administration a gift, with all the money they pay us! . . . And then: Blood comes out easy, all you need is cold water and a stiff brush.

They must be thirsty. A thirst different from the desperate thirst of Sunday afternoons. Hungry. An urge to take over the world. To keep doing things with their cohorts, shoulder to shoulder, no matter what happens.

They probably have to talk loudly, because now we're the ones banging: beating stools against lockers, pots against the heavy doors, spoons against bars, until we sprain our wrists. We need to remind the guards how numerous we are. When they do the banging they strike one bar at a time, one cell after the other. Not in any hurry: silence then clanging, silence then clanging. Silence that reinforces the clanging, like with leaky sinks. The guards move slowly, to annoy us as long as possible. But when the inmates do the banging there's no pause between one clank and another, because while one arm takes a rest there's at least one other, among many, ready to strike. It's exhilarating. More powerful than church bells, more compelling than any car horn or siren, more intoxicating than any stadium or carnival. When you bang, you shake up the things that anger you inside. They're not where they belong. You enjoy waking up the people in town. Call whoever you like! Phone the prefect, the army, the newspapers . . . The prison exists. And tonight you have no choice but to hear the clamor resounding, rising out of its cooped up cages. The prison exists! But when someone is missing, it's like a punctured balloon that deflates. Only the third tier is banging, now, and a few isolated clanks on the second.

On the island Commander permitted cruelty only to keep his men from getting sick, from taking on the immense rage that the island produced naturally, like mold. That's why they forced us to act up. Imagine you're a child: you have dolls, you get bored, after a while what do you do? You make them clobber each other, you make them kiss. That's what always happens. If they're weak, you force them to wear a ridiculous outfit and to touch each other in front of everybody. If they're strong, you make them fight until one of the two stops moving. Or you take a weak one and a strong one . . . Infinite combinations. It was the island's live television. All in all we liked it, too, when we could merely watch.

Commander let it go on but he never participated.

After the uprising the guards would load twelve of us at a time on open jeep beds and drive around for hours, at night, jolting us up and down on those impossible mule tracks. Wooden benches, a freezing cold wind, and others, like you, struggling to hold on and falling over on you. Engines continuously revved up, after all it's not as if they pay for the gas themselves. I kept thinking: Why don't they down-shift? That's what I was thinking. I didn't feel the cold, because in the cell I was constantly cold. But noise is hard to get used to.

Even now, every so often, a noise will scare me, though it makes no sense. A nurse drops a medicine bottle in the corridor, and my blood freezes, I can't move for hours . . .

Then they'd make us get off in the middle of nowhere, saying: Now we're going to shoot you. And I believed it. The others who were with me also believed it. Anything could certainly happen on the island. We couldn't predict that those fake shootings would mean the end of the island, not the end us. At that moment they pressed the trigger. The report of automatic rifles without a round in the barrel leaves an impression that never goes away. It's as though a surge of adrenaline, a huge wave were crashing over your brain. These are things that the guards can only do once, because once word gets around, people don't fall for it anymore. That one time, however, is devastating. It stays with you. Like those who survive with grenade fragments in their brain. I survive with a fragment of a bullet that was never fired. But I don't harbor any bitterness toward Commander. At that time, after what happened with Martini, he didn't count for much anymore; but even before that, when he could have put a stop to the guards' cruelty and didn't do it, it wasn't sadism on his part.

Maybe you should never defend a warden, try to justify him.

Between those who hold the keys and those who don't, there can never be true friendship. They are paid to deprive us of our liberty, and if you try to empathize with them you must have your reasons. You try to understand how they see the world because they no longer see you. To know what they feel, so you can manipulate them. Otherwise you're just pathetic. You're a beggar. You're a pathetic idiot who is convinced of being someone who, in fact, he isn't . . . I never thought I was Commander's friend. As far as I'm concerned, he could just as well not come down here anymore. Some inmates invent imaginary friends, just to talk, I don't. I can stand the silence. But one thing is fair to say: Commander is not a sadist. Nor is it true that he loses his head every time a prisoner's woman is involved. It's that if you let a boy attack a guard and get away with it, you've lost control. You might as well unlock the cells, leave. A guard must be obeyed even when he's wrong, even when he's drunk and licks a photograph; only Commander can punish him. Beating the boy up was good for the guards and, in the end, for us too. It's a form of respect: the boy provoked them, they reacted. It means we exist. Commander let the boy be beaten, not out of viciousness, and not out of envy.

There are places, far from here, where guards have the right to fuck the inmates' women. Prisons where a guard can say: You want your husband to eat? Open your mouth on mine. You want him to spend a few untroubled hours? Hold me, come to bed with me, and I'll give him a mattress to sleep on. I'll move him from under that window, where the water soaks him, I'll give him a blanket. Take your clothes off and I'll give him something to wear.

Here they can't.

Here the worst a guard can do is let the women wait in line for hours on visiting day, and not open the gate if it's raining. Commander never even did that. He fell in love with a prisoner's woman once, eighteen years ago, and got the worst of it. That's it. Regardless of how many things he did, before and after, that time he was the victim, not the executioner. And in fact it's mainly the guards who can't stomach it. Recruits who weren't even born at the time hear the story about Commander and the teacher, and afterwards they look at him arrogantly, as if that were the only thing he's done in his thirty-seven years of service. As if he hadn't gone down into the midst of the rebellious rows when the guards locked themselves in the barracks. It's always the island that comes back up. Indigestible.

Even tonight in the locker room, with the guards euphoric at have beaten the boy, someone must have said: Whenever a prisoner's woman is involved, the Commander loses his head . . .

Because there's always someone who says that. And it's not right. It's not true. They remember you for the worst thing you did. It's the same with killers: maybe you only killed once, but you're a killer forever. One instant labels your whole life. But no one does well, when he's remembered only for the worst thing he did.

When it comes to sex, the guards are as bad off as we are. Even worse. Policemen and crooks are always on TV, but not prison guards, they remain in the shadow: they're the closet where the cops put the bad guys between one episode and the next. And the guards know it. Women know it. The uniform's appeal doesn't cut it. Women know that if a man becomes a prison guard it's because he's failed the police competitive exam, and that he won't ever put the 'Prison Guard' sticker on his car window, or go around in uniform, holding hands with her on days off.

The world considers guards an extension of evil. And so the guards neglect their teeth, and would even if they had the money to care for them.

They drag their feet when they walk. Like us.

The few who have a family are silent when they go home in the evening, or else they yell; and as soon as they can, they slam the door and go out again with their buddies.

The corrupt ones end up corrupting the family as well. The decent ones bring their despair home with them, spewing out the uncompromising, just words they hadn't been able to say in prison.

The only marriages that hold up are those where guards marry each other. Sometimes they marry in uniform—the uniform that others look down on—hoping the uniform will sustain them in the years to come. And by mating with other guards, they've become strange, like a tribe of mountain men.

Recognizable.

On the island many guards let their hair grow and wore an earring. Commander let them do it because everything was peculiar, on the island. A prisoner arriving there would think: In all my years in prison I never saw a guard with long hair; if they can break those rules, they can also break others. It scared them. And that was what Commander wanted. The guards, on the other hand, deluded themselves into thinking that when they took the boat once a month to go to the mainland, looking like that, people would take them for tourists, or someone with a normal job at least. But they had a pistol under their sweaters, and they moved around as a group because in the end a guard never feels safe. And despite the sweater, the long hair and the earring, the girls recognized them for what they were. Every time. We could tell by the way they beat us when they came back. By the desperate way they'd gotten drunk. They'd set out on the leave trying to find a girl to make love with, or at least talk a little, because the solitude made them sentimental, like us. And they'd ended up going to whores, in a rush, all together, an hour before the ferry left.

Commander was not the type to let his hair grow, or hope that a miracle might happen on the mainland. The prison was enough for him.

He decided to handle censoring the mail himself because, at that point, he thought the job was too delicate to delegate it to a mere rank and file guard. Letters are the prison's life breath, and he wanted to monitor every point of contact between the inside and the outside worlds. And he wanted to work through the night, so he wouldn't have to toss and turn too long in bed.

Reading the mail occupied many hours. It's hard to know where a code, a message, may be concealed. Whether an aunt who sends her greetings really exists. If a trafficker really promised his son a scuba mask the day he learned to swim without water wings.

You have to train yourself to read without thinking too much about it.

The political prisoners' women sent nude photos and pussy hair. They wrote: I hope you choke on these hairs, Censor. Political prisoners' women liked to provoke but Commander ignored it. Political prisoners' women didn't concern him, they were from another universe. Because political prisoners themselves were from another universe. The guards shrank before those prisoners. They were uncomfortable even as they beat them. They pissed on the politicals knowing that it wasn't natural, that they were pissing against the force of gravity, against the wind, against everything and everybody, and that sooner or later that piss would spray back on them.

They pissed more out of amazement of being able to do it than out of contempt. Only when they pissed on us were they relaxed. Us, the ordinary inmates. Convicts who are a dime a dozen. Used to calling all guards their 'superiors', even the slowest of learners.

In any case, neither the few brazen political prisoners' women nor the many mortified women of the common inmates created any major problems for Commander. The problems started when a cultured woman, a teacher, fell in love with Martini.

A friend had introduced her to him, by mail, just as Toro had done for the boy. It happens often. This friend knew that there are women suitable for men outside and women suitable for prisoners, and very rarely is it the same woman. The best way to have a woman who loves you and is faithful to you while you are in prison is to choose a woman is adapted to prison. A woman who likes having someone to think about, all the time, from the moment she wakes up until she falls asleep. A man locked up in a cell is the closest you can find to a man in the placenta. Or an imaginary friend who will never leave you. A god. An impotent god who can't do anything about his life, or about yours. All he can do is listen to you. Or talk. An impotent god but also a dangerous one, because he's a criminal.

Women who want men solely to dream about, dangerous but harmless at the same time, are all over prisoners like flies on honey.

Martini was called that because he's one of those guys who are constantly telling you about the beautiful life they had before: cars, women, hotels, restaurants, cocktails, all deluxe.

And about the beautiful life they'll reclaim, intact, afterwards.

Martini would say: I laughed when I robbed and I'm laughing in prison. I always got a kick out of charging into the bank, shooting at the ceiling, and yelling: Everybody down!, and seeing them all drop to the floor. Shooting is the opposite of holing up. The opposite of setting the alarm clock and getting up early in the morning. Foreigners like knives because they're afraid of the blast, but weapons are *supposed to* make a blast. Weapons say: I'm here, what of it?

Martini had a basketball player's body, and he always stood with his legs a little apart, slightly bent, his arms away from his torso. The air of a man who can handle a machine gun with one hand. You laugh more in prison than in many normal lives, Martini said. Once when we opened a safe-deposit box, we found porn magazines and lentils. And that's all. That's the life normal people live! They spend more hours outside, sure, but almost all of that time is spent working or masturbating. One night with three whores, in a luxurious hotel, is better than twenty years with the same woman in a house with a mortgage. And charging into a bank with a machine-gun in your hand is even better. It's a more intense orgasm. It recharges your blood like a transfusion.

If we only count really free hours, I've lived more of them, Martini said.

There's always someone who tells you that the outside world is a prison worse than this one. You like listening to these people. You don't contradict them even when, as with Martini, everyone knows that in life he was primarily a loan shark and a drug dealer. He may have pulled off two or three robberies, if any, when he was young, when he had suppliers to pay. Other than that, he was either in prison or in a bar each and every day, like clockwork, lending money and collecting it, buying or selling, like the banks he claimed to rob. You can say you're freer in here, just as you can say that stepping in shit brings you luck. Though clearly you have more space outside.

The teacher liked her space too. She'd chosen to live outside the city so she could breathe, so she wouldn't see a window a few yards directly across from hers. To get to the school, however, she had to set her alarm clock for 6 a.m. She spent many hours in her car, but later, when her father became ill, she was forced to return each day to the narrow streets of the old town from which she had fled.

After she and Martini began corresponding, she prepared her lessons less meticulously and was less conscientious about correcting assignments. She became more abrupt with her father.

For every ten letters she wrote, Martini responded with one. I don't have time, he told her. And it was true enough. Truer than many other things, at least. People outside have a hard time understanding it, but there are tons of people in prison who have lots of dealings and little time.

After a while, the teacher came to terms with it. What matters is that you listen to me, she thought.

People on the move are always in need of something stationary. More stationary than them. That's also why I'm so well liked by those on the tiers. I'm always here. I'll never be in the yard when they come to look for me in my cell. Or in the shower, or have an appointment at the gym. I'm the prisoners' prisoner.

The teacher would go to places she'd never been to, just so she could tell Martini about them. Sometimes he picked the destination, sometimes they were a surprise. She started recording tapes so she could talk as she walked, without having to stop.

Martini circulated the letters, tapes, and photographs. The only words he censured were those where, replying to him, she quoted things he had written.

The teacher's photographs mainly showed her house. She'd had all the interior walls taken down and had transformed the foyer, living room and study into a single room; because she was alone. But the result turned out patchy, with corners and posts scattered here and there, because the house hadn't been designed that way. Pictures of the other rooms showed a kitchen whose dishwasher always empty, cleaned and tidied after each meal. The teacher also scrubbed the terrace, moving the flower pots to mop away the circle of dirt left by soil and water underneath. She who was always quiet, was forced to hear everything from her neighbors. She, who only made noise when she used the vacuum cleaner late after supper. The inmates idolized her for it. At that time on the island they didn't give you rags and disinfectants, not even if you paid. The inmates imagined themselves there with her, polishing and dusting in that house that seemed like a furniture showroom. A hundred men alone, at the teacher's house.

They asked Martini for photos of the bathroom and bedroom. He decided to indulge them. And she indulged him.

The teacher was pale, washed out, but strong. The inmates knew the difficult things she managed to do and the very easy ones she did wrong. Once the light switch in the bathroom got stuck, and she left the light on for days. She fought like a lioness at condo meetings, so that her common share as a single woman would count as much as the others. But then she didn't know how to change the time on the clock radio. The inmates forced Martini to give her advice. They asked those outside to send her tools and parts. They taught her how to mount shelves, how to lubricate the roll-up shutters.

When the telephone company demanded money it wasn't owed, it was one of them who wrote the threatening letter that set things straight, on letterhead stolen from a lawyer.

She couldn't believe all the things Martini was able to do. Until he told her: It's not just me, there are a hundred of us.

It wasn't sincerity. Martini was constitutionally insincere. He lied even when there was nothing to be gained from it, or when he believed he was telling the truth. Martini did it to up the ante. He told her: Do you know that when it storms, and the mail can't get here, the entire prison becomes frantic? Commander is forced to beef up the shifts, because of you. It's not their wives' letters they're waiting for, but yours. You've become a kind of star here.

He told her that there were guys who touched themselves, that the place was full of men touching themselves while listening to her voice, and that she should be happy about it. That someday he would get out, and they would experience their love intimately. Like everybody else. Better than others. But for now it was ridiculous to pretend otherwise. Right now he had an obligation to his friends and therefore so did she, if she really loved him.

He chalked it up to generosity and camaraderie.

He, Martini, who wasn't generous and had practically no friends.

He enjoyed seeing how far she would go.

For a while she stopped writing. But then she wrote again, as if nothing had happened, without ever mentioning us, or bringing up the subject again. However, now she knew whose ears her voice was pouring into. I don't know if it excited her. Personally, I don't think so. I think she really did it only for him. But many guys were convinced of just the opposite. They said the most awful things about her, and they masturbated even more.

Martini should have knifed them all.

It bothered people who were in love to think that others masturbated too. Only Martini didn't seem to care. One day a group of guys with sweethearts waited for him in the yard and beat him up, that's how sick and tired they were of how little he cared about the teacher. Three days in the infirmary.

Every now and then he seemed to be remorseful.

He'd say: They sentenced me for a load of crap. And for this, my most disgusting offense, there are no laws. He said: You always pay for the wrong crime.

But it didn't last long.

He'd burst out laughing again.

When he found out she was embarrassed to sing, even alone, in the shower, he asked her to do it. This time too, the teacher ignored it for a few days. Then tapes began arriving, with her singing softly under her breath as she ran the vacuum cleaner around. Take this tentative voice of mine, always about to falter, as the most intimate thing I have to give you; for now. That voice exposed her more than a thousand nude photographs. To him. To us.

She wanted to share things with him. He sold them. He duplicated the tapes. Her voice in exchange for cigarettes. Both the ones where she sang and those where she only spoke. Even those where she just read the news of the day. The men who bought them weren't looking for her words, they were looking for her lips as they moved to form them, for the air that had been inside her lungs. In those days duplication deteriorated the quality, the sound became dull, the crackling increased. They bought them anyway. The less money you had, the further away from the original you ended up.

In her tapes the teacher told a fairy tale about an enchanted castle where a curse had frozen time, and where everyone had become invisible, covered with brambles, obscured. Until a hero appeared who was able to see beneath those brambles. She herself was the woman who would make her way to the heart of the castle, she would melt away the time that held Martini prisoner, break the spell.

But the entire castle melted. That woman's heat awakened Commander as well.

Commander could have assigned somebody else to censor the mail, but he realized it too late, when he could no longer do without her. He had to keep reading and listening every day to words that familiarly addressed a 'you' that wasn't him. By then he no longer stamped the letters accidentally, at any place on the page, but chose the words that struck him the most. The ones he wanted to say. The censor's stamp of approval had become his signature, his way of communicating with the teacher. Naturally we only learned about this later on, because at the time no one was aware of it. Much less the teacher.

She asked Martini to read the same books she read, at the same time. But you could only receive parcels weighing up to ten pounds a month, and Martini would rather have food and clothing. In the end they agreed on television. They would watch the same programs, imagining they were sitting side by side, and comment on them in a letter the next day.

The whole prison watched as one. The quarrels over choosing the channels ended. I'm talking about the ordinary inmates, of course, the political prisoners stayed out of the entire affair. The political detainees weren't part of the prison.

And I was in a dark cell.

One night they turned off the TVs a quarter of an hour before the normal time. A quarter of an hour before the movie ended.

It seemed as if the prison would explode.

I have no proof, but I think it was Commander who decided on it.

I think that, over the years, he regretted that base act. But I also think that he wanted to watch the movie to the end by himself that night, just him and the teacher. Because we had all forgotten about the Commander's eyes and ears, which read and listened to the same things that came to us. To them.

Those who go to prison for the first time are usually obsessed with phone calls.

People get sick using the phone; because for sure everybody grips that disgusting gray receiver, they all kiss it; you start the phone call holding it away from you, but in the end you too will kiss it.

Anyway the phone call lasts ten minutes, and it's the guard who places the call. Your loved one will hear the guard's voice first and then yours. And if the one you love isn't home, or if the line goes dead, so much the worse for you. For all of you.

Over time you learn to sense when the ten minutes are up, but at the beginning you're always left with a half-finished sentence. My father never knew what to say on the phone. When he was the only one home the ten minutes felt like an eternity, it seemed like the guard had forgotten to end the call. But that's not possible, because the communication is disconnected automatically, it doesn't last a second longer. Before there was silence about things we weren't able to say, afterwards only silence.

For inmates with good behavior there are award calls, but it's better not to count on them. They're usually given to informers, or those dealing with some hardship. For example, someone whose parents live far away and can never come to visit. The N's get almost all the award calls, but then when it's visiting day they go berserk . . . Anyway, the award calls can only interest the N's up to a certain point, if it's true that they've managed to bring in cell phones.

In the days on the island, cell phones didn't exist. And the teacher couldn't have received any calls, because visits and phone calls were only allowed for family members. She asked Martini to marry her: So we can finally hear each other, see each other. He pretended to submit a request but never sent it. She had to make do with going to see him at trial proceedings. But Martini had already been inside for a number of years, and he hardly had anymore appeals.

It seemed things would go on like that forever.

Yet one day, absurdly, she called.

The guard on duty transferred the call to Commander, and Commander was so overjoyed to hear her that, just as absurdly, he agreed to let her speak to Martini.

That was when Martini began to think that maybe that distraction could become something more. He convinced the teacher to be nicer to Commander: Call to talk just to him. Tell him about your troubles, your loneliness. Say something like: I can't tell Martini this because he wouldn't understand. Put a page or two meant for him in your letters too.

Martini explained all this to the teacher via notes that he managed to sneak out. Because there's always something that escapes the eyes of a censor, the eyes of a commander who, like it or not, is exposed to thousands of words from inmates, which don't interest him, along with the teacher's words that torment him; while his ears remain closed to the most important words, the ones swirling around him.

Martini persuaded the teacher to propose a deal to Commander. She would take a year's sabbatical and come to live on the island, in Commander's house. In return, Commander would assign Martini to some outdoor job so that she could occasionally see him from the windows of the house.

Nothing more.

No direct contact.

To communicate with one another, Martini and the teacher would continue using the letters that Commander would continue to read. No phone calls.

At the first attempt to meet, Commander would send the teacher back home and Martini to the ends of the earth.

The inmates told Martini: You're nuts, the Commander will never agree. He's not a moron. And besides, the teacher's father is sick.

But Martini, being a loan shark, knew that desires blinded people. He knew that if a person believes that he'll get twice the money he needs in a month, it's because need can make anyone believe anything. And helping a person satisfy a need creates an opening. Martini knew how to widen that opening, day after day, until the person had no more room for his own desires, his own plans. Until he became your zombie.

Martini was never a money-lender himself. He worked for an organization. His job was not to earn money so much as people. Make them so indebted that they're forced to do, say, or not say, carry or conceal anything. Even the lowliest of court bailiffs can become valuable to an organization. That was Martini's job: transforming people into empty shells that take orders.

It worked.

Commander began to imagine himself with that woman in his house, and that's all he could think of anymore.

He requested permission from the administration, and obtained it.

I think that even then some within the administration may have suspected. May have seen the trap Commander was laying for himself, and were quite happy to help him fall into it.

The fact is, the teacher came to the island. She took walks with Commander in the evening, along the winding road leading from the harbor to the cannon. The old cannon was the island's only monument and all the free residents met and got together there. Commander was proud to have that woman at his side, it made him feel giddy. He was content. The gravel crunching underfoot, two sets of alternating footsteps. She wore a little silk dress. Nothing obscene, not at all. But silk. None of the few wives that were on the island had a silk dress. The only silk the guards ever touched was that of the fat 'sausages' they filled with sand and beat us with, the rare times when they didn't want to leave any bruises.

Commander respected the agreement and assigned Martini to the most sought-after spot: the new guest quarters. Built on the sea front for exceptional visitors: journalists, magistrates, administration officials. All the best that the island produced, or bought, was cooked at the lodge. Martini did not take advantage of it to become the king of contraband. He told us: It's impossible. Thinking back on it, that already should have made us suspicious.

Working at the lodge allowed him to go to town every day, and enabled her to see him from the window of Commander's house. That seemed to satisfy them.

Commander's authority had plunged to less than zero. Everyone knew that he lived for a woman who in turn lived for one of us. It was uplifting. One of us carried more weight than a commander and a teacher put together.

And on top of it, Commander was now reading books.

Inmates who went to make the bread or unload food supplies at the port or mow the grass at the guards' gardens, saw him sitting on a bench, sometimes on a rock.

Commander read because he was in love.

And he was in love because he read.

The books, however, like the teacher's letters, weren't meant for him.

A prisoner is fooling himself if he studies, and there's a chance he'll get hurt outside. As long as he's in prison, however, the others respect him. That's how it was at one time at least. For a warden, however, it's different. No one will respect him because he reads.

Commander even put on glasses in those days.

In prison 20/20 vision was never of much use to anyone.

Maybe for those on the perimeter wall, who knows. Everybody else lives and works in close spaces, where 20/25 is more than enough. In prison it's much safer if you don't see too well, and don't wear glasses, in case they slap you. Even now that they hire people with degrees as guards and they almost never strike you, even now those who really need them prefer contact lenses.

Only the political prisoners wore glasses, or the very elderly.

That year Commander wore glasses. He didn't really need them, he was still young. At least young compared to how we are now. He started wearing glasses because he associated them with reading, with his desire to become a different person.

That was a strange time, for Commander. He did things that weren't like him. It was a prison undergoing restoration. Nothing is as vulnerable as a prison being renovated, simple to escape from, full of forgotten tools, of scaffolding that tomorrow, certainly, will make the walls more solid, but that today makes them easy to climb over.

When the books the teacher brought weren't enough for him, he resorted to the prison library, in the old infirmary, kept in rotting fruit crates. It was mostly church stuff. But also a few novels that had landed there by chance, and technical manuals from when the island was an agricultural settlement: sanitation, surveying, construction. Books to transform the world.

If one was out on loan, either he had it or I did.

They called us 'politicals', behind our backs, to make fun of us, because back then the political prisoners were the only ones who read.

Which was a dangerous crack to make. At that time, assigning the same nickname to an inmate and a warden was in no way a compliment, and it was not without consequences; we would have been forced to react. Luckily, we only found out about it later. fund

When someone escapes, the guards become enraged. It's as if someone had raped their wives under their noses. They feel like fools and *cornuti*, cuckolds. As for the island: the prison's reputation was spotless, few escapes, constant deaths at sea.

The day Martini didn't return to his cell, Commander felt doubly foolish and *cornuto*.

He thought: My job is over today.

Starting back in guard training they teach you that, in prison, you should never forget to lock up. If someone leaves his locker open, the entire group is confined to the barracks. Because you have to learn that man serves the lock, he is the extension that enables locks to function. And should the day come when all the locks were to fail, the guards would have to link arms through the bars, steel themselves, become insensitive to being slashed. As in the story of the boy who puts his finger in the dyke and resists, his finger freezes and still he resists, because if he didn't all the lands would be under the sea, all the mills, farms, animals, blond women in kerchiefs would be swept away.

Commander was determined to do just that. The most noble part of his job, the ability to be tough and fair, indifferent to threats and flattery, unassuming as a lock. Invaluable for anyone who is on the other side of a door that shouldn't be opened. Because evil exists, Commander told me that many times. It walks on earth, among us. It can't be extinguished, it must be walled in, to prevent it from spreading everywhere. And if at some point you can no longer distinguish it from good, it's entirely your fault: evil continues to exist, to be different from good, to walk among and trample us.

You need places to contain evil.

Keys to lock up those places.

Men who can withstand the incandescence of those keys.

The problem is that there is no lock, no matter how well made, that cannot be opened. And the worst thing of all is that a lock that has been opened and closed again is indistinguishable from a lock that has never been opened. A wall can rot, crumble, but it will never deceive you. You can trust a wall, not so locks and people. They're the prison's weak point, the concrete's decay.

On the day of the escape, Commander submitted his resignation, but the administration refused to accept it.

They found Martini that same evening, hiding in a cave, with enough food to hold out until they gave him up for dead. Until someone could approach by sea, to retrieve his remains.

Those who saw the cave, a four-hour walk from the prison, swear that it was impossible to spot, no matter how many men, dogs, or helicopters were sent out. Evidently, someone had continued to keep an eye on the teacher even after Commander had stopped. In the year prior to the escape, she spent less and less time at the window and more and more time walking and swimming, until no one paid attention anymore. They considered her part of the landscape. Or at least so she believed.

They say that the fact that he fucked her was what blinded Commander.

I wouldn't be so sure. I know you can live side by side for months, without anything happening.

What's certain is that in January the teacher went to the mainland to visit her father. And Martini escaped.

Commander expected to be transferred at the very least. Instead, the internal investigation determined that it had all been carried out from the sea, which was certainly true, and with that the matter was closed. Yet no one had ever been able to pull off anything from the sea without assistance from the island.

The administration knew, yet they kept Commander on the island. Where everyone remembered. Where he would continue to be embarrassed forever.

Maybe the administration preferred a commander who was weak, drained; maybe it had decided to continue where Martini had left off: to take over the zombie.

And when they shut down the island, they transferred him here.

And that's what worries me.

We live in a prison commanded by a man who is indebted.

There's a room here, not very big, with eight white plastic tables and four chairs around each table: three white and one red. Imagine the outside of a very cheap bar. Except that the room is locked. From the windows you can see the prison yard.

Visitors enter and sit on the white chairs. The empty red chairs await the inmates.

Seated on the white chairs are women and children. Fathers or brothers are more likely not to understand or forgive. Or maybe they're inside too. Or sick, or dead. It's a fact, they have less endurance. When they arrested me I thought: If nothing else, I'll have my father back. Because that's the way he was, he was one of those people who, if an acquaintance becomes ill, begins to spend more time with him. He liked sitting beside someone who was lying down. Handing him something to drink. He had no friends but he visited a lot of people. With me though he couldn't do it. He came a couple of times; on the ferry he puked his guts even when the sea was calm. Then he got sick. It took him five years to die. Other fathers simply get tired. What's the point of wasting all that time, all that money, to then spend an hour feeling uncomfortable?

So male voices turn up in the visiting room all at once, when the inmates arrive.

At first the noise is that of a kindergarten.

The kids are overexcited, because they've been eagerly awaiting the visit for days and weeks.

My little niece looked forward to the visit the way kids in other families anticipate an outing, or a toy. It's important for children to have a focus, a promise for the future. On the days leading up to the visit, they went to the market: my mother, my sister and her little girl, to buy food for me. A whole section of the fridge was filled with the finest stuff, for me. Nobody touch this cheese, it's for *zio*. And I was just an uncle: imagine when it's for a father. There are weeks when the kids compete to put things aside. Because that section of fridge is daddy. Putting things in there is like feeding him. And the more you feed daddy, the bigger he grows, until the cell will hardly hold him, and it will be easy to spot him, even from a distance. But there are weeks full of boredom and anger, when they'd like to eat it all up and not think about it anymore, and only when the sofa is covered with washed and ironed clothes do they realize that yes, the next day they're leaving. The inmates' clothes are either all dirty, in a big bag, just back from a visit, or all clean, arranged on the sofa the day before leaving. They're never half-dirty and half-clean, scattered around the house.

The guards are sexually more frustrated than we are. They have the right to fondle empty clothes, not those with women in them. They shake, touch and stroke the shirts, with the excuse that a rigid collar can conceal anything. They put their fingerprints between the woman and the prisoner. But the women, after a while, learn to smooth out the shirts again, on the spot, with their hands, imparting their fragrance so that the inmate doesn't notice anything.

But then, why am I telling you this? I don't have children and my niece won't come anymore. Still, I know everything there is to know about prison, even things I didn't experience first-hand. Because in prison there's time, a lot more time than there are things to tell. I know that outside, beyond the outer wall, while their mothers wait in line to enter, the kids sit on the ground, drawing. Then they draw in the waiting room, until they really can't stand it any longer, and then they throw their crayons away and tear up the paper, and all they want to do is go home.

They're half-asleep because they're usually woken when it's still night, at four or five in the morning.

The women pick up the crayons and salvage the drawings that haven't been ripped up.

The men stride in, cocky, as if it were a parade. Being watched, day and night, some have become convinced that they deserve it. That they are interesting when they shit, when they sleep and when they walk.

The women remain seated, because they know they are not permitted to get up.

Most of the children keep running around.

The men are nervous. If they've been called in, it's because someone has come for them. Yet they look around, fearful that someone else, someone quicker, has sat in their red chair.

Then, slowly but surely, each man finds his place.

Some of the children refuse to sit on daddy's knees because they're convinced that the man locked up is staying there on purpose, not to come home. But it's easily resolved. All the man has to do is say: Try opening the door. And the kids get up, go over there, fumble around, bang on the door, and finally realize that the prison door is impossible to open. Only the guards can do it. The guards who, in there, are the only real adults.

The kids have a good cry and go back to the table.

The women cuddle them, pallid.

That pallor should reassure the men locked up: I don't go out, I don't see anyone, I don't see the sun and the sun doesn't see me. As if the things people feared the most didn't happen in the shadows . . . The truth is, that pallor doesn't allay jealousy, but envy. I'm having a bad time too, believe me, their pallor says. My life is also disrupted. I'm not allowing myself anything: I'm waiting for you. I'm suffering.

They dress modestly, the women do. So as not to risk attracting any comments, not to force the men into a brawl the next time they're out in the yard. At least that's the way it was at one time.

But the ones who are dressed worst of all, who are more pallid than anyone, are the guards. Standing beside the doors. One guard at the door leading to the outside world, one at the door that sucks you back into the heart of the prison. At one time you recognized the detainees because they were all dressed badly, all alike. Now it's the guards who are badly dressed, all alike. Scratchy woolen uniforms, with buttons that are too big, too silvery, too chipped. Black safety shoes, which are not found in stores and which no arch support can make pliable. Shoes that no one would ever buy, because they're used to clomp around in a prison. Miles and miles and miles, in the bowels of the earth.

The guards are pained by the women.

They watch them without understanding.

What are all these women doing here?

Why are they at the railroad tracks, in big cities, when it's still night?

What do they want from these men who have left them alone?

Beautiful women, waiting for hours to embrace those men for a moment.

And they come back, again and again and again.

Men who can never support them. But these women don't seem to care at all about the future, or the past. About those other fathers, children or mothers, about the other women their men have ruined or killed.

The guards fill their talk with the victims. Some are sincere. Obsessed. They actually see an extra chair, at the visits. A transparent chair that's always vacant.

From a small side room, through a darkened glass, a guard contemplates the absences in the visiting room.

And the women. What matters now is holding hands.

The women show the men the children's drawings, saying: He made it for you. It's not true, he did it out of boredom. But it doesn't matter, the drawings will still get hung in the cell. Always the same drawings, in all the prisons of the world. There are houses with the whole family around and arrows pointing to the names. Because otherwise you wouldn't know who was who: without arrows and without names you couldn't tell who was the father, who the mother, the child, the grand-mother. They're all small. Sometimes the father is drawn smaller than the children. Because he is impotent, con-fined, needy.

The men gather up the drawings and take out their own. Almost all the inmates draw. The guards think: When did you ever draw, outside? Now they draw. They write home every day. It makes them feel like parents, doing that. Now they call their wives and children: Love of my life. Instead of getting on their knees and saying: Forgive me, forgive me all of you for making you have to come here and see me in this condition, like a dog on a chain . . . They urge the children to study, they shout loudly to overcome the noise the others are making, they play at being the head of the family. The guards think: I know what you do in the cell, from morning till night, you don't even watch the news . . . yet you sit there, boldly, and urge them to study. To always obey their mother.

Obey the woman you left alone.

To stop thinking, the guards study the inmates' hands.

Hugging and kissing on the cheeks is permitted at the beginning and at the end of the visit. During the visit they're allowed to hold hands.

And contraband is passed through hands.

Not just the guards, but the lovers, too, focus on their hands. Hands become very sensitive, over time, since they're the only way you can touch. And hands that are stared at intensely convey even more. They're bare, and they can embrace each other as much as they want. Embraces that stand in for the whole body.

I've always had my visits at a counter with a glass partition, like at the post office. I've never had any problems respecting the regulations. I would have liked to have the little girl touch my face, sure. But I had no other temptations. For lovers, however, if there's no glass it's torture. Usually they are appropriate when they initially embrace, because they don't want to be denied the visit; then too, at the beginning, there is always some awkwardness. You look at the other person, but it takes a while to realize that it's really her, she's really here . . . It's the final embrace when they go all out, because they've had time to get reacquainted. Sometimes they kiss on the mouth. They think: There are eight couples here, they won't single us out. All eight couples kiss on the mouth.

The guards go crazy. They start banging the keys against the microphone. Keys that are eight inches long, heavy as rocks, a goldish color, so you can see at first glance how precious they are, radiating freedom. But they're brass. Troublesome to carry around, to insert them, turn them. Only good for clanking against the bars or against a microphone. They make a hell of a clatter. It feels like they're clanging right into your eardrums. But the couples go on kissing.

The guards worry because a lot of things can be passed from one mouth to the other and easily swallowed.

When someone kisses, the guards call his name out over the loudspeaker: Martini! What are we doing? Do you want to lose your visitation rights? Control yourself, control yourself . . .

Because the prison where Martini was transferred, on the mainland, permitted visits from third parties, and the magistrate authorized the teacher. There was no reason she shouldn't be. She didn't appear in any of the investigation reports. Naming her would have meant naming Commander. So as far as the administration was concerned, she did not exist. And she could show up to visit every week.

She and Martini sipped soft drinks, held hands, and sang.

They sang together the songs that she had recorded on the tapes for us, a long time ago.

Those who don't know Martini can't understand what it's like to imagine him singing at the visits, holding her hand.

A lot of people thought: He's using her. Who knows what he has in mind this time . . .

But this time Martini didn't let anyone read her letters.

He never mentioned her. All he said was: I'm lucky, very lucky.

Sometimes he railed at her: I can't stand it anymore, having to thank you. Owing it all to you. It's horrible. It's something that destroys a man.

He raised his voice.

Before they never fought, because he didn't care.

Now, though, they sometimes had to write to each other as soon as the visit was over. She, hopping mad, on the bus that took her back to the station, her words distorted by the bumpy road. He, on his cot, to apologize.

It's normal. For a visit to work, it takes a bunch of words written before and after. Martini and the teacher, however, had an advantage: they didn't have an intimate past relationship to mourn for, taken from them by prison. It was all still new for them, still to come.

At the end of each visit they kissed on the mouth, not giving a damn about the guard.

I knew a guy who, for quite a while after he got out, whenever he kissed a woman, was afraid that someone somewhere would suddenly start banging keys, making a hellish racket; that they'd call out his name saying: You're going too far!

And another guy who, in contrast, could only make love in a hotel, with the door slightly open, because by then, for him, the risk of being censured was part of sex.

Modesty is a strange thing.

Martini and the teacher were unperturbed.

There are places where, after an unauthorized kiss, they send you to the ends of the earth, without notice. On the day of the visit, the guard at the gate gets the satisfaction of telling the woman: He's not here anymore, he's been transferred. Where? I don't know.

But that didn't happen in Martini's prison. He and the teacher went on kissing, visit after visit.

And hearing the voices of children all around them.

Martini stopped having shivers and staying in bed when they injected him with interferon against hepatitis every fifteen days. He got through the whole winter without a cold, and in the spring he asked the teacher to marry him.

She said yes.

A lot of people said: So that's what he was aiming for! Since he'd already served more than half his term, having a wife and a home waiting for him, outside, would make it easier to get probation . . . In the judge's mind, a wife and a home would compensate for his old escape attempt.

But I say: he had only four more years to serve, why put on such a farce? Four years fly by in a flash. Prison can be comfortable, for those who are used to it. Probation, on the other hand, can become very, very complicated. And Martini knew it.

Especially if you go to live with a woman who has never lived with anyone.

Was it worth it?

I think Martini was sincere.

Anyway they got married.

The kind of ceremony they have in prison, where they don't allow you to drink alcohol even on that day. Martini ordered a beautiful cake, but at the last minute they said it couldn't be brought in, even though he had filled out all the applications requesting permissions for months. The administration decided that it was up to the prison to contribute the cake. Maybe they were acting in good faith. Certainly they reminded Martini that he couldn't choose anything, inside, not even the shape of his wedding cake. And they let him give her a single, lingering kiss without banging any keys. Then they brought him back to his cell. The teacher, still dressed as a bride—not in a traditional bridal dress, but a dress bought for the occasion at least, that she would never wear again—she, dressed as a bride, went to pick up the cake they hadn't allowed to be brought in. And gave it to a nearby community center.

The witnesses had thrown rice. Rice all over the concrete floor. In the squares in front of town halls or churches there are always drains, potholes, steps where rice can hide. But on the cement floor of the prison it bounces around and then waits to be crushed underfoot or swept away.

Martini, however, had the good grace not to complain.

He would be getting out sooner or later. Sooner rather than later.

There are some who get married behind a glass partition, and are serving life. He in a small room, she in another, and between them a glass wall that even sounds can't pass through. Like a sound studio, or a control booth. Reflected in the glass, the bridegroom sees a transparent image of himself, superimposed on the bride. They talk through a phone. They say I do, they cry, while what they hear on the other end of the line is an artificial voice, minus any high or low tones. The phone is worse than not being able to touch. Yet they go on with the wedding ceremony through the glass. The bride is dressed like a sugar-paste figurine on a cake because everything has to be extravagant to overcome the glass barrier. They kiss through the glass, touching their hands together on it. They cry like babies, each on his own side. They cry some more and throw more rice than at a normal wedding. The grains smack against the glass, like flies, bumping into something they can't see. It's a force that hurts, and drives them back, and they don't know what it is, yet they continue on.

These things happen, in the world. They've happened, and will continue to happen. There are tens of thousands of people who only communicate with another person six hours a month, through a glass. And there are manymore who wouldn't have anyone to fill those six hours with. That's why even someone who gets married through a glass usually has the good taste not to complain. I know a lot of people, inside here, who would have a hand cut off, I mean seriously, just to have it touch someone else's on the other side of the glass, six hours a month. Anyone who says the visits are torture is talking bullshit and knows it. Including me. Never forget it, because if you complain too much you might come to blows with someone who, maybe, has kids who for ten years have refused to answer his phone calls. For ten years he's been eating the things that others receive from home, without ever being able to reciprocate. People who get visits and phone calls are part of an elite no matter what. You can suffer, when the visit is over. But you must never forget, even for a moment, those who don't experience that suffering.

Word has it that tonight, at the 4 a.m. head count, Toro looked up. Not to provoke: out of inattention. It was the first time they'd woken him for a count, after so many years. If they want to count you they can just as well do it while you're asleep. When they decide that everyone has to stand there, hands behind his back and eyes on the ground, it's because they want to break you. They want an angry prison, full of people who haven't slept and guards who have been working too hard.

Toro forgot to keep his eyes lowered. So the guard approached. Toro stared at him, not understanding. And an instant later he got slapped. What are you looking at?, the guard said to him.

As if he were the lowest of the lowest.

Obviously the story can't be true. No guard would ever slap Toro like that, so light-heartedly. Many things may have changed, but not that many. When it's time to close Toro's gate, the guards slide it slowly, so they won't disturb him. Toro didn't get slapped, and they didn't find tears on his pillow, at the 8 a.m. count. It's absurd. Everyone knows it's absurd. But it doesn't change anything, what matters is the rumor going around. There are prisons where the guards are required to check if there are tears on the pillow and then report it, because if someone cries too much they either put him under observation, to prevent him from killing himself, or they suggest he become a snitch. Or both those things. It's all the same. Anyway at our place, thank God, it's not like that. Here only your fellow cell mates check for tears. And if they are true friends, they worry about you, if they're bastards they tell the whole prison. But the boy who lives with Toro is not a bastard. A more unlikely story than the one about the slap and the tears had never been heard . . . Nevertheless, Toro will have to do something. He has no choice. Reputation is everything. The smaller a place is, the more reputation counts. Here it's not like you can avoid it, go around it, let it go. In a confined place, if you let it go one time you've lost, for good. Even I, when I killed, did it for my reputation.

This morning Toro came down to the yard with the boy, supporting him, because he still can't walk.

Toro's eyes are scary. The more fear you generate the less violence is needed; it's a tool of the trade. If he went home and forgot to change his expression, his little son would burst into tears. Today, however, Toro came down without an intimidating mask. Focused, hardly looking, like when there's nothing left to decide and all that matters is dealing with things in order. He and the boy walked around the yard, then asked the guard to go back up. That walk cost Toro a half hour's struggle and pain for the boy. They were followed, a few yards back, by all the men on the second tier, whispering to one another. Like at a funeral. When he buried his son, Toro forbade a procession of cars and scooters. He forbade any display of weapons or, worse yet, shooting in the air. He wanted a quiet funeral, going on foot to the countryside through poorly cultivated vineyards and poorer harvests. In the past, in Toro's village, the wine barely reached eleven degrees; people went around shooting carelessly. A person could end up spending his life in jail for killing a murderer who, without knowing it, had offended another murderer. Now the wine is fourteen degrees, controlled by oenologists who sell it all over the world. And practically no one is killed anymore. Yet so few years have passed since the afternoon when Toro picked up his son and carried him over his shoulder. It's best if the weight of those who no longer have life falls to the fathers. Washing away the blood can be done by the street sweepers or the rain. But it's best if the weight is borne by someone who isn't doing it for the first time, and knows how to hold him, set him down, arrange him to look like himself. People watched from behind closed windows, the way they're now watching the N's. The N's now call the boy 'cow' even in public. What's the name of the bull's wife? Cow.

Up till now Toro hasn't reacted. Maybe he's waiting for orders, in organizations you have to be able to wait.

He only asked the attendants for a new mattress and, with the boy, started hanging silver foil from cigarette packets on the walls again, to reflect more light and make the cell seem bigger.

When the guards beat someone up the way they beat up the boy, afterwards they usually transfer him elsewhere. Maybe Toro is simply incredulous at having the boy still with him.

Who will attend Commander's funeral?

A warden or guard, when he retires, survives between two and five years on average. Less than a miner. Rarely, when he comes out, does he find someone waiting for him. He's very close with his colleagues; by banding together they reduce their fears, slow down their heartbeats, as when diving underwater. But the prison quickly forgets those who leave it. And the guards, unlike us, can't go back. Not as guards, at least. A party, a gift, and off they go. In three years it will be Commander's turn. He spent his life protecting those outside, even knowing that there was nothing for him out there. He could have bought a little apartment in the city, with the money from his overtime and from the vacations and holidays he didn't take. A small apartment suitable for a man alone, with no empty rooms. But Commander isn't used to things that are the right size for him. He's used to things that the administration provides. It's the man who has to adapt. The walls can't shift just because a man without a family has slept in the commander's quarters for some ten years.

He goes out riding his motorcycle every night but then he returns to the prison.

Better that than coming back in the morning and stopping in front of the gate, uncertain. From his windows Commander sees them: the few guards who live in town. Every morning it takes them forever to walk through the intermural area. Entering and exiting the prison is as difficult as changing time zones. And from his windows, on the side facing the yard, after an expanse of several yards, Commander also sees a floor identical to his, populated with cells. When he can't sleep at night he knows that, for every step he takes, across the way there's a man lying down. And below, in the guards' barrack, there's another. Commander's living room is as big as a cell for twelve men. It holds a desk, a chair, and nothing else; he never sits there.

Every night someone is making love, in the prison. And someone is making love outside. Where Commander lives, on the borderline, nothing happens. The floor of staff apartments is empty. A deputy was never appointed and the chief accountant chose to live in the city.

Better to walk.

Take off the pajamas and put on the uniform. Or maybe sleep in the uniform. The beauty of being in charge of a prison, for a man alone, the beauty of sleeping in a prison is that if you die in your sleep someone will come looking for you the next morning. If you wake up, however, and the night isn't over yet, you can get out of bed and find someone to talk to.

The guards have to talk to you, you're the highest in rank.

And often they do so willingly, because in a prison solitude is the norm; and that's also the beauty of it, for a man alone.

You can walk for hours, always indoors, through illuminated corridors that are never-ending.

A shadow appears on a screen in the control room, disappears for five minutes, then reappears on another screen. Or it doesn't reappear. Ghosts. We've always had too few video cameras here. And black and white monitors, fuzzy, cloudy like the eyes of old people. Prison has always existed among these mists and ghosts. The colors and clarity of new video cameras would sound a false note, here. Deceive you into thinking that the prison, and everything in it, has suddenly emerged into the open, into the sunlight. It's not true. And it would be dangerous to believe it.

If he were a guard, they would already have assigned Commander to the perimeter wall.

But a commander can't be sent to the perimeter wall. He can shut himself in his office and sit at a desk in front of flags that have never been in the wind, or he can make the most of it and work a little at night, because the prison has doors of flesh, weakness and nostalgia, which open at odd hours. The trouble with wanting to talk is that what you didn't tell the guard who was drowning you in salt water, you'll maybe tell someone who leans against the slot in your cell door and offers you a cigarette, just when you need it most. Commander has always talked to me, even knowing that I'd never informed on anyone, and that I'd killed one of them.

Well aware that if a guard speaks with an inmate for no specific reason he risks being seen as the prisoners' friend, and he will never shake off that label. No one will sit next to him in the guards' mess hall. No one will offer him a beer. Even the inmates will begin to treat him badly, because they know they have carte blanche. It's as if a guard who is a friend to prisoners had no colleagues: no one will move a finger to defend him, you can say and do whatever you want to him.

But Commander's reputation is both too highly regarded and too critically regarded to care about such things.

He can go on walking around forever at night, with his eyes closed, in the corridors of his prison.

He never got lost, until two months ago.

That time, though, he forgot where he was.

Whether he should go up or down. Keep going or turn back. Only I know it. The video cameras didn't notice a thing. Because if a commander walks through his prison, and at some point stops, goes back and suddenly turns around again, there is no way of knowing if he's lost or if he's simply making the rounds again to check on things.

Maybe I shouldn't tell. It's a little spiteful. But I haven't seen him for a month. You end up getting vindictive, it's inevitable. And those dogs never stop barking. And the food trolley is late, not even an attendant around so you can ask what's going on . . .

I can recognize Commander's steps. I knew when he went by the examination room, the infirmary, and the passage point. To the gate leading to isolation. Or when he went up to the tiers instead. Today I don't hear anything anymore, no steps approaching or moving away.

When he walked through the prison at night, Commander's boots thumped in such a way as to not awaken those who were sleeping, but to warn whoever was awake. All the considerate, or simply lazy, guards do so. There are a few perverse bastards who approach with a light step and at the last moment speed up. Most of the guards are relieved to hear a rustling ahead of them, someone holding his breath, fake snoring, then rustling again, a dozen cells back. Because if they see something they shouldn't, they're forced to step in, and most of the time it isn't worth it.

Commander still thinks about it.

He never told me, but I'm sure of it. We've all been deceived, once or twice, but he's one of those people who can't accept it.

At this moment, as the gates and cell doors throughout the prison slam shut in the empty silence, Martini is at home with her. He opens and closes doors whenever he wants, wooden ones, not armored doors. Assuming he hasn't died in the meantime, because when you're inside, it doesn't matter where, even at the ends of the earth, there's always some news; all the prisons are in communication with one another, they are trees without leaves but with deep roots, and the roots talk among themselves, and the earth is weakened by these channels that meet and embrace underground, under asphalt highways, marble office buildings, empty pool bottoms . . . Those who are free don't realize it, but they live on a thin layer of perforated, crumbly soil. They too can be swallowed up at any moment into the world down here. But I don't think Martini will be. He's too old. I think he will actually live out his days with her, crime-free. He who never had anything in his name. No car, no house. A total tax evader. Never voted. Now he has a home.

To persuade the magistrate to release him, the teacher explained to the neighborhood's residents who he was, how long he had already served and what they both still hoped for from life. And on and on, until the neighborhood signed a petition: We are willing to accept him. With his first and last names on the doorplate. Martini waited in line at the registry office to obtain his identity papers, and the clerk couldn't believe that a man of sixty had no previous documents, not even an expired one. As if he were just born, the prison's certificate in place of the hospital's.

Here many are obsessed with dying a grand death. Especially those who tried to live a grand life and didn't succeed. The blaze of a grand death, instead of a small flicker that is snuffed out . . . That's why there are some who say that Martini should have died with a weapon in his hand, even if it were only a sharpened teaspoon. Died on the perimeter wall, climbing over it with the certainty of not making it.

Here people are obsessed with a grand death in order to forget the dreaded one, in the infirmary, with those enormous eyeglasses they give everybody, which look like safety goggles but are just poor man's glasses. Each individual has his own illness, but they give everyone the same identical pair of glasses; and they comb their hair with the same comb, to do the job more quickly. Then the younger inmates push those who are able to sit in a wheelchair over to the bars, to expose them to the light. The latter try to look out, but it's too late. They have a hard time focusing. As long as you're still going out to appeals, you should focus on the distance, they say it's good for the vision; ignore the things around you, which you never notice, and stare at the horizon. Practice. Nobody does it. The old guys here become blind, albino and transparent. Like certain snails that live in the dark, at the bottom of grottoes, and are identical to those on the surface except for their skin, which looks like gel. You can see what they eat, the digestive path. You can see all the internal organs, but nobody sees them because it's so dark.

Was that a sound?

I have the feeling that there was a sound, but when I woke up it was already over.

Fortunately, the prison is here, waiting for us. If you wake up with your heart pounding, maybe because you dreamed you were being chased, or were with someone who's gone, the prison will help you until your breathing returns to normal. It holds you up, off the ground, fixed to the wall with your cot. It senses your movements. While you sleep, the prison wonders: Is he okay? The prison holds its breath to listen to your breathing.

On the island I threw feces at the guards, as everyone does, so they would come and beat me. But the guards are slow. You can cut yourself, you can yell, they come when it's convenient for them. If I had clothes, I stuffed them with paper and stuck them in the toilet. I sealed the crack under the door with my socks. Then you pull the water chain, keep flushing . . . Gradually, the cell gets flooded. The water rises slowly, like time. Like rain. Like an afternoon that lasts for years, with neither night nor morning. Up to the ankles. Any higher than that becomes tricky, it begins to filter out into the corridor. But up to the ankles is already lots and lots of water, even in a tiny cell. When the socks are suddenly removed, the entire tier is flooded. But that's not to say that the guards will come quickly, even then. You summon them with water. Your liquid emissary. And if there are other inmates, they summon them by banging against the bars, yelling, excited by the water flowing out and by the brawl that will follow. But that's not to say that they'll come. Only the prison itself is always there. With its bricks and stones within the concrete walls. Clay. The old prison, before they completed it. It warms me to think of those stones, and the boys who hauled them up, to build the reformatory that would lock them up. They say that a prison built by inmates must inevitably contain a secret. It's unlikely that anyone would readily work to build his eventual, perfect place of captivity. They say that there is an escape route under the grating at the edge of the big yard . . . So they say, but no one has ever tried it. The guys throw pebbles down there and are scared off by the echo. They say: If no one has ever tried it, it's because it can't be done. That's not true. If no one has ever tried it, it's because they've all been too scared. Of the dark, of the close space, of insects, solitude, death. I've lived with those fears for years, if I haven't gone into the grate it's only because I don't believe it. The boys built what they were told to build, period. The only thing they left us is the warmth of the stones buried in the center of the walls. Stones carried up from the quarry in their arms, as they staggered along; a few fell, sometimes disappearing into the sea like a dead weight. Wood, or wool, quickly gives you a feeling of warmth . . . but only stone preserves it.

Such silence, now, in the pipes . . . It's improbable, in a prison with a hundred guards and four hundred inmates. On the island, after I killed the guard, I heard the water flushing so often that at a certain point I was sure they were doing it on purpose. It was during the time when the guards made a phone ring and ring for hours in front of my cell. I was going out of my mind. I heard the water flush and I thought: They're doing that for me. They're doing that *to upset* me, and I can't retaliate. Because at the time I was in an empty cell, with a concave floor and a hole in the middle; they brought me water in a bucket, along with the food. You could try to beg for a little more, but it was pointless, you only risked having it poured on you.

Here, instead, after a while you fool yourself into thinking that you control the water.

But it's not true.

You have no more control over it than you do over the rain falling outside. On the island Commander used to say: In a prison that functions well, detainees decide nothing. When you open the tap you're not really turning on the water, you're asking. And if the answer is no, you remember that there is a valve somewhere that separates you from the water of the mountains.

When they shut off the water it's usually because a serious search is coming, with dogs and guards from outside, not the impromptu rage on a Sunday night. Often that's how you find out about it: you go to wash your hands and no water comes out. And a moment later the corridor is full of shouting guards. You try to get rid of all the things you shouldn't have, but that's just why they shut off the water: to prevent you from making them disappear down the drains.

Sometimes the search goes on for days, and the prison's smell changes.

When the dogs from outside come in, our dogs in the intermural area bark until they choke themselves. They don't bark at us or at the mice, they only snarl; since they know us, they're not alarmed, they just wish we were dead. But when they see the drug-sniffing dogs go by, they leap against the chain-link fence protecting the entryway, sometimes cracking their teeth, and hang there, slobbering, bleeding, while continuing to bark. The more the other dogs ignore them, the more frenziedly they bark.

I like the drug-sniffing dogs. They do a fruitless job, because whoever orders the search usually already knows where the drugs are, and turns the prison inside out just to avoid getting the informer who told him in trouble. Basically they are snitch-protecting dogs, but I like them anyway, because after one tier they're already tired, confused. Bored. It's not true that they drug them to train them: they make it into a game. Finding the drug is like playing with the trainer. But making the rounds of a prison, cell after cell, floor after floor . . . They tug at the leash, wanting to leave. They're so bored they'd even let us pet them. It's the guards who won't permit it. There is a dividing line between inmates and dogs that only dogs are allowed to cross. You have to wait for them to be the ones to sniff you, as part of their job. Whenever

I hear a search team coming, on the one hand I'd like to cover up, to protect myself from the men's blows, and on the other I'd like to remain naked, to feel the dogs' breath on my legs.

Martini was the kind who, each time he returned from the hospital, told you how pretty the nurses were, and that he got a boner whenever they changed his catheter. I never believed him. They only touch you with sterile gloves. And with syringes, or at worst a lancet, which is basically a knife. We're used to dealing with knives, only juveniles still use their hands to beat each other up. Here you assume you won't use your hands a lot, but you expect that when you get out they'll be important again, especially if you're weak or sick. Anyway, it's not true what Martini said, as nice as the nurses may be, they have to wear gloves, in accordance with regulation. That was another reason why straddling the guard while I was killing him was upsetting: on the whole because of the physical contact it suddenly involved. It had been more than two years since anyone touched me, except to handcuff me. Wearing gloves. Even when they handed me the white plastic cup, full of water and medication, or a letter, they used latex gloves.

Once, as a child, I happened to pet a dog with a latex glove. I remember it, it's one of the many useless things I remember. I had found him in the street, he could have had mange, who knows, his fur was missing in places. We only kept him in the house for one afternoon. On that afternoon my mother said: You can only touch him if you wear gloves. So I put on the thin kitchen gloves, and the dog, who when I found him was dying to be petted, suddenly stopped looking at me. Petting him like that or running a brush over his back was one and the same.

On the island, when I killed the guard, it had been two years since anyone but the barber had touched me with his bare hands, since he too was an inmate, and instead of giving me pleasure, it bothered me. Better yet: it made me uneasy. He touched me with the comb and scissors, but every so often his fingers grazed me, and it was torture, because it doesn't take long for you to become unaccustomed to contact. But a dog would give me pleasure. It's nice to be with a dog that doesn't want to tear you to pieces. When the dogs in our intermural zone close their eyes, they dream that the maintenance people left the door leading to the outside entrance open. They dream of running and finding the inner door wide open as well, of entering the concrete-enclosed exercise yard with an unbounded leap and finding it teeming with us, despite the darkness and the night; of finally being able to sink their teeth into the life within us, after countless days, months, years of longing.

I understand them, the intermural dogs.

They live in a cramped corridor, set between a forty-five-foot-high wall and a thirty-foot high facade. They run in an empty gully. It's natural that what they crave most is to see something appear that gives some meaning to all that running, something to kill.

They accept food and water only if those are lowered over the wall.

From outside.

The dogs seem to know that there is no way to scale the wall from inside the prison, not even for the guards. The only access is from an outside tower. That's why the weapons are kept there: so that we can never get to them. And that's why the dogs only accept food if it's dropped from the wall: because they know that many of us, inside, would like them dead. They know they're locked up in a place where nobody wants them; it can't be easy. Still, it's not easy to have to wait for a search to be close to a dog either. Especially when, like tonight, the search doesn't materialize.

The guard had come to get me after two years and two months in solitary.

Being ingenuous, I thought: They're letting me out because they know I won't talk. Letting me out meaning they're putting me in with the others, free to walk outdoors in the big yard. The sun was shining. I thought: They could have been spiteful and waited for a rainy day, but just look at that cloudless blue. The vast sparkling yard. The sky high above, and the clouds even higher. And all those people cheering me and clapping their hands, from behind the bars.

I breathed. I directed my gaze at a distant point, at the end of the soccer field, and I felt dizzy. From the windows, from behind the grilles, they were applauding. The guys who worked in the laundry had come out, all of them, and they too applauded. I kept walking, following the guard. Proudly. They put me in isolation to break me, and now they're releasing me because they gave up. They're the ones who conceded.

I was twenty-seven years old. Twenty-four of them spent out in the world. Then seven months on the side of a mountain with the Coffee Princess. Three months outside again, transporting things, then two years and two months in solitary. And now the reward of that endless yard . . . At some point, however, the applause stopped. It took me a moment or two to notice it. There was a bit of wind, I thought: It's blowing the other way. It's diverting the sounds, but the hands are still clapping.

Instead, there was silence. Total silence. And that's never a good sign, in prison. Then I looked around and saw that we were walking toward the south exit of the yard, toward the infirmary and those in protective segregation, and not to the north, where all the others were.

I froze.

At that time they used to play those little tricks. If you don't talk, they spread the rumor that you talked. Or they move you to protective custody, which is the same thing. It's a way of telling everyone: He's an informer, he's afraid to go back among the ordinary inmates. And of telling you: You might as well become an informer for real now, because going through that door into protection brands you forever, there's no going back. Nobody here would think to doubt it. What you say doesn't count for anything, it's just talk. But the walls where they hold you do count. If you're within the informers' walls, you're an informer.

When I realized where we were heading, I dropped to the ground. I started crying.

I got on my knees before the men who were watching me from the tiers.

I yelled that none of it was true.

The guard seemed uncomfortable. Apparently he wasn't expecting it.

Could that be?

More importantly, he didn't seem to realize that the yard, in which I had never stepped foot, was in any case more mine than his. Because a prison, unless it's brand new, belongs to the inmates. Guards with a minimum of experience know it: prisons absorb contraband like sponges. In an old prison you can search everyone from top to bottom before and after any transfer, but you can never really be sure of what they have on them, because the older prisons get, the more porous they become, full of crannies, peculiarities, hidey-holes. And the older they get, the more they pity us, their children. An inmate always has a map of knife locations in his head. I knew that there usually was one in the tubing of the bench on the side of the yard. It's information that is passed around. Screaming and weeping I ran to that bench and grabbed the knife, while the guard kept looking at me without making a move. He seemed worried about the noise most of all. Worried that Commander, hearing the uproar caused by my yelling, would think he was incapable of even such a banal assignment as transferring someone from one part of the prison to another. And that it could create problems for him, afterwards. But only a rookie would take for granted that an internal transfer is something simple. And assume that there will be an *afterwards*.

Thirty-five times. The rest of the prison was shocked. They knew that I had never killed anyone. Or even wounded anyone. Above all: I had never been beaten. Someone who has never been beaten remains fearful.

Never more than a spanking from my parents. At school I had always managed, in one way or another, not to really get beaten. I didn't go out in the street often.

That leaves you fragile.

Never having had the living daylights beaten out of you, and seen that it's nothing serious, leaves you with a basic weakness, a willingness to give in. Others can read it on your face. That's why they were shocked at how I attacked the guard and killed him, and killed him, and killed him again, thirty-five times.

The ones on the tiers don't realize how much rage is built up in solitary. Those guys talk, play cards, eat together . . . Before I killed in the yard I had already killed a hundred times in my head. I was brimful, spilling over, bursting: I was spewing death. I killed the way a geyser can kill. There are some who do it because they feel empty, a ghost among ghosts, and hope to finally find strength by killing; not me, for me every blow was like stretching. I extended and opened up beneath the sky, and the knife helped me penetrate farther, take up more space. I was excited to have an excuse to do so. Snuff out a life to expand my own, make more room for my life by taking another. For months I had dreamed of nothing else, literally. The blade went in as if sinking into a cushion, something soft, full of almost nothing but air.

Pulling it out was different.

Especially when he stopped struggling, and the body came up with the knife. There I felt the effort, the weight. The body gurgling. You shatter a life, with your hands. You think that something must remain attached to you, like phosphorescent pollen after you pluck a flower. Instead there's only muck. And then the fear that the blade may break. The certainty that they would shoot me, from the perimeter wall, before the job was done. Instead, they let me finish. I don't know how long it took me. Minutes, for sure. I kept stabbing. Because, though I'd never killed anyone, I knew—people had told me—how hard it is to die, and how the blows are never enough. The human body will have none of it, if its time hasn't come. There are some who have survived twenty, forty thrusts. I gave him thirty-five.

From the windows they kept yelling, as if possessed, as if they were sexually aroused. Like sharks around blood.

At first he struggled a lot. That was to my benefit, of course. The more he thrashed about, the faster the blood gushed out of the cuts. The beauty of stab wounds is that they don't cause pain. What was previously joined is now separated by an invisible wall of air, and the person who is inhabited by that wall experiences no pain. He knows he has to move, do something, or he'll die. But every movement intensifies the bleeding, draining him . . .

At some point I straightened up, to get the kinks out. Because it's true that I always did push-ups, in isolation, but the muscles weaken a little anyway. Not to mention the tension: I was a bundle of nerves, rigid. I started feeling small cramps in my arms, my back, around the groin. Because I was straddling him, I was gripping him firmly with my legs. So I got up, I waited.

Nothing was happening: the guards still hadn't appeared. I paced, I walked around. I heard how they were yelling from the cells. So I crouched over the guard again, to satisfy them. Twice I stood up, twice I bent over him again. Even though by that time I was the only one there. Just me, and some flesh on the ground.

From the cells they went on shouting. So I stooped down to stab him again, feeling no pleasure, like pricking a sausage with a toothpick so the fat will ooze out while it's frying.

When the guards arrived, it was a relief.

I couldn't take it anymore, I didn't know what else to do at that point. Even the guys behind the bars were bored by then.

I thought the guards would kill me right there, on the spot. Instead, they took hold of me and brought me back to isolation. And in the days that followed, they built the wall and left me in the dark. But that doesn't matter much. What bothers me, what doesn't give me a moment's peace, is how long it took them to come while I was stabbing the guard.

Afterwards I tried to think about him as little as possible. I didn't know him; it's worse for a man who kills his wife. But when you've killed only one person in your life, and you killed him like that, hand-to-hand, grappling with him, the danger of magnifying it in your memory is very great. As with an only child, a one and only love, anything that's unique . . . A one-time killing. Toro himself doesn't even know how many he's killed or had killed; it makes it easier to have a composed attitude.

I killed only that one guard, and I killed him while sitting on him. I felt every move he made. I had to resist, by force, the jolts of his strength, of his life that was seeping away. But I didn't let it bother me: I didn't spend my nights dreaming about him afterwards. It was necessary; I would do it again. Plain and simple. He was very young, but I too was quite young, and killing him cut short my life. Either him or me. The smaller a place is, the more the choices are reduced. What continues to torment me is the idea that they let me do it. And I don't understand why. Why didn't anyone shoot? Asking Commander would be useless. He's a sober person, discreet, he never forgets his role, even when he's talking to you through the food slot, in the dead of night. Besides, at that time he was actually under the administration of an external commissioner, after the episode with Martini and the teacher. Maybe not even he knows why the guards took so long to come. Taking someone out of solitary is dangerous, always; it's like sticking your arm into a dark hole. Why, knowing that they were going to pull that trick on me, moving me to protective segregation, why did they send only one guard? And why didn't they order him to handcuff me? They didn't even instruct him to search me. A new recruit from training school . . . So unprepared. He didn't even know what it *means* to transfer someone to protection.

The more I've thought about it, over the years, the more certain I am that they made me kill him. Every now and then, for mysterious reasons, the guards want to kill one of their own.

And they try to get us to do it.

This makes me regret what I did.

It should have been my triumph. My being God, for a moment or so. The way I'd imagined it a thousand times, before and after. Heard it told a thousand times. How when you're about to kill someone, that person gets down on his knees, begs you, wets himself, shits in his pants. Listens to you. For him at that moment you count more than his mother. Then you take his life. They are sacred moments, serious. Time stops. The light is transformed. That is, the first time, of course; afterwards it becomes routine, but the first time there's you, the victim, and the world that stops. And if he doesn't plead with you out loud, it's the same thing: you know that inside he's begging you. And his plea makes up for all the times you had to beg for a cigarette or a change of underwear, a pencil to write with . . .

In other words, the beauty of weapons ultimately is their threat. The sound when you load them, the sensation of momentous things to come. And I didn't threaten anyone. I never aimed the gun at the Princess, never pointed the knife at the guard. Right into his flesh, quick work.

I dream about weapons often. There are those who are raised in families where at some point they give you a gun, and you're not really grown up unless you always carry it with you, against your skin. You get so used to it that after a while you're no longer aware of the weight or the cold sensation, and you go around armed even where you shouldn't, and maybe you get yourself arrested that way, stupidly. Not me. I never thought about them before, they were never important to me.

I had a normal childhood. My parents always signed my exam book and checked my homework. Always put my lunch in my schoolbag. Only in prison did I start dreaming about weapons, and mourning, in my sleep, the ones I don't have anymore.

Or never had.

In the dream, I pull the trigger to shoot, and make the sound of the shot with my mouth. And pray that the victim will agree to fall. Like kids. They have to go along with it, otherwise they won't die, they go on standing there. They show you that your weapon is worthless; they take it, and walk off. I try to block their way, hoping they won't go around me, that they won't ignore me like they ignored the gun. And I make the sound of the shot again, louder. Flashing the weapon.

The weapon must be believed. That's why some people buy bigger ones than they need. The weapon must be believed and the man must be believed. Because a judgement about the weapon is always a judgement about the person overall. If they don't believe you, you have to shoot. If they do believe you, you don't: then instead of shots there's silence; or rather, words. And respect. They'll describe you as standing taller, afterwards. And everything you say will be noted. They'll never tire of listening to you.

They told me about a kidnapping—they're always telling me about kidnappings—a woman who was well treated, held in a farmhouse. When they knocked to bring her food, she'd reply: Come in!, as if they were waiters. Then one day they went in, pointed the gun at her head and said, You're not in a hotel, lady; we knock to give you time to put on your hood and turn around to face the wall. When you're done you have to say: I'm ready!, not Come in! You're not giving us permission to enter. You obey the order we give you by knocking and when you're done obeying, you say: I'm ready.

And from that day on things changed.

The gun balanced out the woman's money.

At some point she even started asking the kidnappers to stay, after supper, to talk a little. I didn't need weapons with the Princess, but there are cases where guns make talking easier. That's why some families put them in the kids' schoolbags. And that's why some thieves become talkative and polite during bank robberies. They say: Sorry for the disturbance, no one will be hurt, now we'll do this, all of you please do that . . . And this money, ma'am, whose is it? Does it still belong to the bank or is it now yours? Because if you've already signed the withdrawal receipt we don't want it.

And everyone thinks: How cool-headed! Such a level tone of voice, *during a robbery*. And they don't realize that outside of the robbery he would have stammered. It's the weapon that enables you to pronounce clearly, to pause, in front of someone who otherwise would interrupt you. If I had a gun now I could go on talking forever. Killing the guard, on the other hand, I was merely someone else's instrument. I didn't hold the weapon, I *was* the weapon. That's the thought that torments me. And that, yes, I regret. The suspicion that I did the guards a favor.

You could have done anything, outside: raped, dealt drugs, killed wrongfully . . . The guards really only punish you if you have harmed one of their own.

Or if you've tried to escape, which is the same as harming one of their own, because they consider the prison one of them.

It's understandable. The world doesn't care much about what goes on in here. And in here no one cares much about what goes on outside. Only if you kill a guard do the other guards feel duty-bound to hurt you. It's a way of protecting themselves, of honoring their fellow guards. When they meet the widow, or the orphans, they want to be able to say: We're getting back at him.

To punish me they built a wall. The isolation cells were more or less the size of these, nine by six feet. They halved mine. I no longer slept perpendicular but parallel to the door. The window and toilet remained on the other side of the wall, out of reach. There was nothing on my side anymore. No light or air from outside. Not even the concrete cot. Nothing at all. There was only me, naked, and a hole in the middle of the floor. And a bulb overhead, shielded and turned off. And the darkness. So dark that you can't see your hands. That you have to touch your eyes to know if they're open. So dark you can't be afraid, because there are no shadows, no sounds, no monsters. Only food and water that every so often, abruptly, are thrown at you. Food. And you have to pick it up from the floor before it reaches the hole. Darkness. The utter, endless darkness before birth. The utter, endless darkness afterwards. At a certain point there would be cascades of colors, fluid, like fireworks. Because your body can't stand being without stimuli for too long. All you have to do is press your eyelids with a finger and your eyes explode. See things that aren't there. Or maybe you get insubstantial fragments, that come from who knows where, who knows when. Because in the end we are made in a merciful way. Rightly so. What is taken away from you is somehow restored. I had never seen such intense colors before. No mountain sky like that, no matter how sunny or windy or how early in the summer it was. Maybe only in drawings made with felt-tip pens, as a child. Or not the drawing either: the color on the tip of the marker, still glistening with alcohol, before being transferred to the paper.

The problem is that the guards know it.

When the cascades of colors appear, they turn on the light. And they leave it on forever. The cascades disappear. The emptiness of your cell re-emerges, with the shielded bulb, high above. And the hole in the middle of the slightly sloping floor, made of concrete like the walls. The whole room, your coffin, converges toward that hole. The only way out is through there. You envy your feces. You start throwing them around, because it's the only thing you have, the only thing you do, and the bulb burns your eyes. I threw so much shit at that light, to make it a little dimmer, more kindly. More humane. But it's useless. So you sit down, hugging your legs to your chest, your head on your knees. You embrace yourself. Squeezing tight. And hope that the cell will embrace you, and that the prison will embrace the cell, and the island the prison, and the sea everything around it, with its darkness. You long for a little darkness. Who would have said it: your worst enemy, up until the day before, and now you're begging for it, just for a few hours, to counter the light, to counter the guards paid to spy on you. You close your eyes and hope to become invisible, the way kids do. But real darkness doesn't return. There's still a reddish glimmer in front of the eyelids. You would need several hours of darkness and several hours of light, alternating.

That's what you need, but it's hopeless. Instead, they give you days of darkness and centuries of light.

And they tie you up if you throw too much shit around.

They bring a bed, finally, but only to tie you onto it. A bed with a hole in it. Whatever comes out drops directly onto the floor and slides toward the center. From your hole to the prison's. All you can do is scream obscenities, try to spit out the food, or bite the hand that shoves it into your mouth. You're an infant. But if you do that, they can close your mouth and force feed you with a drip. Then you're an old man. You're back in the dark, you're nothing. They can't do anything more to you, because there's absolutely nothing you can do.

But it's not so.

There's still time. You can pay with that.

When a situation can't get any worse, they can still prolong it for you. Even blind, mute and unable to move, you pay with what time does to you. You draw from a reserve without knowing how much you have left. You pay a month, and you don't know if you've paid a millesimal share of your life, or a much greater part.

I was saved because at some point they brought other people down.

The island was at a boiling point: they had started distributing the punitive bread. Almost every day someone was sent down. It was impossible to talk to the new arrivals, they were too far away, at the opposite end of the corridor, but I heard them screaming when they broke down. It gives you strength to know that someone hasn't been able to hold up. He couldn't take as much as you did. You suddenly feel like you're worth something. There's one thing at which you're better than others: resisting, not losing your mind. Then when the guards realized that I was resisting, that the emptiness and the light wouldn't kill me, they started beating me. And making the phone ring for hours in the corridor. They listened to music with the sound blaring. But once again those idiots were mistaken: because by the way it reverberated, the music reminded me that not all the cells were empty at the far end of the corridor.

They beat me without covering their faces, wearing their ordinary uniforms, since beating me up must have been a routine thing. Nothing to be fearful of. There was no danger of running into me, later on, in the prison yard. Or worse yet: outside. I would remain locked up forever. Solitary forever. Theirs forever. So there was no need to assembly a squad, plan a time to beat me up. All they had to do was get up from their desks, whenever they felt like it, as if going to get some coffee.

Many against one. Clubs against bone. Boots against bare skin. If you're naked, and they're wearing boots, it's almost inevitable that they will kick you. The foot, the boots, lash out on their own.

Sometimes when they left I got hard.

I'm not ashamed: I know it's happened to others as well. It's not masochism: it's the relief. You get an erection and you masturbate, without images, without fantasies, you try to create an emptiness, in silence, outside and inside your head. Silently because any sound could make them come back.

I'm hungry.

I started feeling cold, and scared, twenty years ago, in the woods, along with the Coffee Princess.

On the island I was even colder, and more scared.

I would pull off a button, throw it on the floor, and bend over to pick it up. Then throw it again. It keeps you busy and keeps you from sleeping as much. Because sleeping on concrete, in the winter, is bone-breaking. But if I was naked, and there was a hole in the ground, it was hopeless. I stayed cold.

Hunger, however, real hunger, never.

Over the years the fear went away. The cold remained. Now the fear is back, together with hunger. This business with the food trolley . . . I can't move, I call out, and the food doesn't come. I yell, but the prison has stopped feeding me. Where did it go? You can hear the crash of the sea. Maybe the prison killed itself, maybe it jumped into the sea and left us on our own. How long has it been since they brought anything? Two days, three? How do I measure time without food . . . Even outside there are a lot of people who live for meals. They talk about shopping, they cook, set the table, eat, clear away, wash the dishes, set the table again, eat again . . . They eat slowly, to consume time together with the food. Here, though, you notice it more. Here you measure time by the food trolley, even if you can cook in your cell, or have a clock. Now I can't measure it anymore.

I'm scared. I'm ashamed to say it. Yet if I didn't say it, I would be even more ashamed. I'm scared because I have hope. Because, absurdly, I feel like I still have something to lose.

It's true that I have life without parole, but laws change . . . Then too, there's always pardon. I said: I know my life is over . . . Well, it's not true. No one has more hope than someone who has been locked up for so long; if you don't kill yourself, you develop faith in what's to come. It's inevitable. Like an interior grotto, where hope seeps out. A secret reserve. It doesn't rain, because it's not in contact with the world. But neither can sun or wind dry out that little trickle that slowly accumulates. Drip by drip. One drop per hour. Thousands of liters in dozens of years. A lake with no sky, but full of hope. I'm more ashamed of being hopeful than of being scared. When I quit smoking ten years ago, the guards made fun of me. What are you lengthening your life for, they'd say. I replied: I'm quitting because I don't want to be in need of money for cigarettes anymore. I don't want to have to sell myself for that, some day. And they believed me, respected me. They stopped making fun of me. Whereas it would have been better if they had continued, because the truth is that I did quit smoking to live longer. Those who say that being in prison is like staying at a hotel are wrong, because nothing dries up hope like a hotel. There are many people outside who kill themselves when they pass fifty years of age, because they realize that the world no longer expects anything from them. Except an inheritance, maybe. Here instead, with a life sentence, you think everything is still ahead of you at age sixty. That you can become an astronaut, a dancer, an entrepreneur. Because you have so little behind you. As if the things that make up life were in a sack, and you can't see what's in it but you can feel it's heavy, and in any case, if you've drawn so little out, something must be left in there. All the life that hasn't been lived must, somehow, be saved up somewhere. Still to come. It can't have evaporated simply by pacing and sleeping. Maybe with a death sentence it's different. I don't know, I've never met a man condemned to death. I heard a program, on the radio, about the last meal: they choose the same crap as always. They take the holiday menu and multiply it by three. Triple portions of all the spiciest, most revolting dishes that you can have when you're locked up. Some guys ask for ice cream and a cookie, or a basket of assorted candy, and nothing else. I thought: Maybe they don't remember what you eat outside. Then I thought: Maybe they do remember, even too well ... They're fulfilling desires left over from birthdays of long ago. A kid's menu: fizzy, fried, sweet, salty. Pizza, whipped cream, orangeade and meatballs, until they throw up. A hundred pounds of candy. Like those old men who die calling the nurse mama. Or maybe it's not that they remember too well or not at all: they've never known anything else. They entered prison when they already stank of bad food, having been born to mothers who stank of bad food. Five fried chicken thighs!

I'm hungry.

When you're hungry all you can think about is food.

Only at the end of the program did they say that prisons are now authorized to spend very little on the last meal. Many don't even grant it anymore. That is, they don't let the prisoner choose. It was a superstition, they say. A way to try to mollify the condemned man and persuade him not to come back to haunt you afterwards. But the guards are no longer afraid. They tell him: You didn't offer the victim a meal, we're not offering you one. Drop dead, period. Kick the bucket and be done with it, there's nothing we should be pardoned for!

Guards are obsessed with the victims.

They picture them outlined in chalk, on the floor. Even if a victim never fell, even if there was no shooting, he wasn't murdered, but may simply have been cheated, kidnapped or mistreated.

A chalk outline, empty inside, like constellations.

I have to stand by that outline, Commander used to explain to me. Keep it visible, even after the rain has erased it. The prison walls are the continuation of that outline and I, with my footsteps sounding through the corridors, am the continuation of the walls. And you killers must remain empty, like that outline.

The more things they deprive us of, the more certain they are of honoring the victims. And it doesn't matter if, in their zeal to deprive us, they also deprive the victims of something. Because I know that the victims' survivors are full of questions which only we can answer. With their lives mangled, struck by a bolt from the blue, they keep returning to the scene of the crime. Why? Why did you have to kill *my* husband, *my* son, didn't you know that I existed, that I loved him? And if I had known, would that change anything?

I knew one, a victim who wasn't mine.

He was in prison because he had committed several crimes, but he was also a victim because they had killed his teenage son. Another juvenile had waited for the boy outside a bar and sprayed him with bullets, with the frenzy of someone who is new at it and doesn't want to miss.

This victim that I knew . . . Well, at some point they gave this victim the opportunity to approach his son's killer in prison. They did it on purpose. The fact that it was his son's killer was a secret. Only the father, the magistrate, and the killer himself knew it, no one else. To this day no one knows, only me, because I'm down here and it's as if I didn't exist. They decided to make the two meet, what's more, to put them in the same cell together, certain that they would kill each other and that it would start vendettas, retaliations . . . Who knows why. Evidently, for some reason, the administration wanted it that way. Sometimes they're glad if you kill someone. Whatever the reason, they served the killer to him on a silver platter. But contrary to expectations, the two stopped coming down to the yard and spent hours talking. Days. Non-stop. Killer to killer, because the father had also killed and ordered people killed. They exchanged gifts.

It's impossible to understand.

No one knows what they said to each other.

Maybe the father asked him about his son, what he remembered about him. Sometimes, to kill someone, you first have to follow him around, find out all about him. Stay close to him. And this father, this victim, had entered prison when his son was ten years old. A son left as a boy and killed when almost a man. The killer could tell him something about that life he hadn't shared: about the people his son spent time with, the things he liked, what his habits were . . . Or maybe the killer said: All I knew about your son was his motorbike, and the bar. I would have shot anyone who got on that bike that day in front of that bar. It happens. Maybe he noticed the father's disappointment and offered to tell him about himself, instead. After all, he and the son were more or less the same age, it's likely that they would do more or less the same things . . . For sure the victim clasped the hand that had killed his son. They remained in the cell together, the father took care of the young man, made him study. He found him a girl. And it's lucky that the man, this victim I knew, had already separated from his wife. Otherwise he would have even shared the dishes she brought from home with the killer. And she would have cooked them, not knowing anything about it. Because even between victims, between a grieving father and a grieving mother, it can be hard to talk about. It's difficult to understand what sorrow does, how it works, how it erodes, who it unites and who it separates.

And a magistrate, on the other hand, thinks he knows, and stops my letters.

The Princess and I lived through a fundamental experience. It should be up to her to decide if she wants to talk about it, if she wants to recall it with me or not. We share an intimacy, forever. More intimate than any husband with whom she is probably continuing to have kids, one after another, heaps of kids, kids who by tugging at her earrings and forcing her to wear low heels, have maybe kept her from quickly becoming too grand a lady.

The dogs seem closer to me now.

Both fainter and closer.

As if they'd managed to get into the prison, but the wind has weakened them. This is a wind that blows downhill, a wind that rises up over the mountains and then, as it rushes down, heats up. It's rare for it to make its way this far, into the basement. Yet you can hear it through the heavy cell door that no one locked for the night; it drags up the dirt that no one has swept and exits through the grate, swirling away toward the yard. People who are locked up like wind. With wind, even those who are stuck in place have the impression of moving. When they brought me to the hearings, I would get off the ferry before everyone else, like a minister and his entourage. I got on last and stepped off first. Surrounded by cops, cars that talked to each other via radio, helicopters hovering in the sky. In prison I was a killer, in the courtroom a mother's kidnapper, but there, on the dock, it was all for me: the dark sea, the wind, the police. The power of the state. Handcuffs aren't shameful when you stop traffic. You feel ashamed on the highway, when they make you get out at the autogrill, to pee, shackled with four other poor bastards like yourself. I was euphoric when I got to the courtroom. Only when I realized that she wasn't there did I feel a little let down.

I saw several members of the band for the first time at the trial.

I also saw people in the audience, strangers who insulted us. Some came every day just to insult us.

The only person I didn't see, the only one I wasn't able to speak to, was her.

During the two hundred and twenty-one days of the kidnapping there were just the two of us, on the slope of the ravine. The courtroom, by contrast, was jammed with people shouting and gesturing, under a towering vaulted ceiling fitted with floodlights, like a sports arena. What could she know about that courtroom?

I went to prison with few memories.

Outside there's no time to look back, only as a prisoner did I learn to remember. At the beginning you raid those memories, you take what you need, at a given moment, to make yourself feel better, or worse. The first times, the last times. Exotic vacations, events. But one memory recalls another, then another and another . . . If they realize that there's a void, inside you, they flock en masse. They're untamed, wary. They duck away quickly. But if the first ones, the strongest, find nourishment, they slowly drag along the weakest ones, the most timid. The whole enormous herd of memories advances, inhabiting you. The years in prison filled with the ones that played out earlier.

I've never had a good memory. I remember houses, rooms. I'd like to remember which cabinets in which rooms, what kind of things were wrapped in newspaper and stored under, or on top of, a particular cabinet, left to gather dust. To be forgotten. The kitchen where we embraced for the first time, dancing, what were the tiles like in there?

It's an activity that, outside, usually occupies old people.

The advantage the elderly have is a body that is weakened, better suited to stop the consequences of memories. They have quivers, not real movements. And when the shiver isn't enough, the surplus becomes tears. Bodies that are rarely used, however, fling themselves all over the place when a memory is sharp, causing harm.

If I were to go back and walk the streets of my town, the people who met me would scream. Sometimes I dream about people I used to see, who didn't know one another, and in the dream they've become friends. The world moves on, even in dreams. The wound has healed over, but people are worried. The person who took my name plate off the letter box, who burned my bed, knows that someday I could return.

That's why others dream about me the way we dream of the dead.

I have a good relationship with the dead. I understand their anguish. I know what makes them suffer. If I don't try to talk with my mother, it's only because too many people have been locked up in here, before me, and they'd interfere. People who have been appealing all their lives, and would start up again at the first opportunity. The requests of the dead, the forms printed in bloc letters.

My mother helped me with the memories, while she was still alive. She brought me something every time she visited. This spared us many of the problems that arise with those who persist in wanting to talk about the present, or the future, and end up reproaching the other for not being there anymore. I retained little about the early years, of course. Children leave their memories to their parents and rarely, as adults, do they ask for them back. Instead, they make new ones, as if they were children again. I however had to ask, with my eyes lowered, and my mother didn't hold back. And if she didn't know, she asked around about it. People didn't want to remember me, but the more they tried to avoid her, the less she could care, and she went on probing.

Now I have no one anymore.

She's buried, I'm buried.

I could contact her, of course. The light of the dead to illuminate the corners into which I struggle to see. They can be unbiased, the dead, even when they've loved you. They don't only tell you what you want to hear, and that's important, in order to remember. In five years, if I'm still alive, I will have spent more time inside than out. By now on I've scraped together whatever there was to get from outside. I rummaged through the garbage. I happily dug up scraps of life that at first seemed useless, or disgusting, to me.

I dusted them off, as best I could, and kept them with me.

Now there's nothing more to find.

The Coffee Princess is still alive, I think. With her it would all be easier. Talking about the days we spent in captivity, inside the plastic tarps, on the side of the ravine.

My voice keeps me awake. I talk loud. I complain about the noise and then I yell, but I've spent too many years with the cell door closed, and in here, unless you shout yourself hoarse, nobody hears you, you have to keep repeating, shout even louder ... Or maybe I'm just getting deaf. And that would be a big problem, because while a blind prisoner can still hope to survive, if you're deaf, sooner or later you'll disrespect someone. Misunderstand a critical order ... Or something whispered word-of-mouth that could save you. I wear headphones when I listen to the radio. This makes me even more deaf, but I like the faint voice that filters into my ears, especially at night. I like documentaries, but all in all I'm okay with any program, as long as it's talk. As long as someone is awake with me, and stays awake afterwards, when I fall asleep. I like traffic reports. Traffic and weather. Clouds a thousand times bigger than the prison. Highways, interchanges, toll booths. There are places that, when I hear them mentioned, bring back the days I drove the van. They mention them, even though there's never any traffic at night, never any backups. They name the places to tell you that nothing is happening. Like a circulatory system without blood. You travel from a sleeping prison through a sleeping countryside. Illuminating animals on the side of the road that quickly bound away.

With the hunger and silence I dream a lot more. That is, I wake up more often, with a start, and I remember more dreams. I wake up in the middle of them.

I dream of being at her house, in the Coffee Princess's living room.

When I said that after a while you only dream about prison . . . It isn't true.

And I don't think that the wound has healed over. I hope that there is still a wound, somewhere, a wound that remembers me.

Even when I'm daydreaming I picture us at her house.

With her husband and children. I don't think we'd end up in each other's arms. An irresistible attraction, like an inclined plane. No. Solitary hasn't been enough to make me that soft in the head. She's the last woman who was close to me, sure, but I know that her life has continued on. I imagine us having tea, finally properly seated, well dressed, clean, with gleaming cups and tea-spoons, in a warm place. Absurdly at her house. I imagine one of those lovely, one-story homes that you see in magazines, with a designer fireplace, a spacious, half-empty living room, a huge window beside the fireplace, and beyond the window lush green trees. Because they had money after all, maybe not actually the Coffee King's, but anyway they had it. And I certainly didn't manage to get it from them. I imagine one of the children running in from another room from time to time, from some part of the house that I can't see, and interrupting us. Her husband sits in a corner, like a kind of waiter, but the children are constantly passing through the room where we're talking.

I miss children. I've always talked with them through a glass partition, it's been twenty years since a child has touched my face, stuck his fingers in my eyes.

Here, prior to last year, before everything changed, they had even planted a small park for those visited by young children. In the intermural area. Two families at a time, in the summer, away from all the ruckus, from the woes and odors of the others. A strip four by ten yards wide, alongside the vehicle entrance. They blew up the concrete, and poured new cement, a foot deep, because there's no way the garden's soil can be in contact with that of the outside world, for security reasons. And there couldn't be any trees, because they'd block the line of fire from the guard towers. The grass had that one foot for its roots, but it was enough: the lawn grew, it was watered. The park was fenced in, to protect it from the dogs that otherwise, at night, would have destroyed everything. They would have chewed up the little tables, the chairs. Anyone with children under the age of twelve could request to have their visit there, in good weather. Those who were able to do that told me that it was delightful, without all the noise. Sometimes you could hear the children's voices all the way down here, below ground, on the other side of the prison. Because their voices have a frequency capable of passing through walls. So while it's true that there was no sunlight, because there's never any sun in the intermural area, they still enjoyed it there.

Until last year there was also a carpentry workshop here, a theater ... It didn't even seem like a prison. It felt like a college. At least, that's how I imagine a college. The doors of those on the tiers were kept open eight hours a day in winter, ten in the summertime. They could leave their cells, wander around. They enrolled in everything. You'd ask a guard: Where's so-and-so? And he'd reply: I don't know.

Then they covered up all the grass again, and you could hear the dog's nails skidding on the cement. Now there's not even that. The dogs liked trotting around. They were ecstatic to wreck their nails knowing that earlier the area had been forbidden grass. Its mark was left, in the cement: the dogs saw it, we saw it. I can still see it. It's not true that time wipes everything clean. Not even in prison.

Soil remained beneath the cement.

Soil that had deluded itself, like earth dug up at a worksite on a highway.

Soil that had been sleeping since they built the prison, that breathed for a year, and that must now sleep another hundred, another thousand years. But sooner or later it will return to the sun and rain.

And in any case, in obscure ways, it continues to live. In the dark. With plastic spoons that have remained buried. Forgotten toys. Worms. And it waits. More patient than us, or the dogs.

The prison's big orange light is out.

It's never happened before.

They'll notice it from the town, from along the entire coast, for miles. I can see the cement is dark, beyond the window. The power has failed several times before now, but the floodlights on top of the poles had never gone out: they have an independent power supply, backup generators. Because a dark prison is an ungovernable prison. In a single cell darkness makes the walls seem thicker, but in an entire prison it dissolves them. They should call in the helicopters right away, to provide light from above. Have them fly over from the cities. The guards should be running around, yelling: Lock up! Lock up! Barricading themselves in the toilets. They should be shooting from the perimeter wall. The dogs should be barking. The inmates, too, should be looking for one another, calling out to each other, wrecking things. Instead men and hounds are silent.

You hear the sea, you hear the seagulls, fraught, frenzied, as if there were no more garbage; or as if there were heaps of it, unattended.

Cell doors banging for days, without rhyme or reason.

The silence, the screeching.

They must be talking about it on the radio, but without power the radio doesn't work. There's still water, thank God.

It would be a chance to see the stars, from the windows on the tiers, but the sky is overcast. It wouldn't be as dark, otherwise. On the island, during the revolt, it was clouded over. It also rained, and I didn't look for cover. Then the army came and turned on the floodlights, and you couldn't see the sky anymore. But it was intoxicating just the same.

The Princess's children must have completed college by now. The more the years go by, the harder it is to update my fantasies, to imagine a Princess who has aged. It doesn't work. It's like in those movies where in the last ten minutes they make the protagonist look old, to show how he ended up, but underneath the make-up you can see that it's still him, still young.

The only person I saw change through the years was Commander.

I can wrack my brains but I can't imagine the kind of experiences that transform people. The choices, regrets, successes, failures, encounters. Here only the body degenerates, slowly but surely, like a leaky faucet. Here you fall apart all at once, one hundred percent, when you enter, so later the problem no longer comes up. Prison doesn't care about the details, it doesn't question every single thing. It tells you: You're nothing. And leaves you wondering whether you can be anything. Afterwards. It forces you to keep thinking about an afterwards, even if you have no hope of getting out. I too think about it. A lot of guys, here, yammer on about tropical beaches. They're convinced that tanning themselves in the yard is enough to prevent them from being recognized, once they're down there. They have no money, their legs are swollen, streaked with broken capillaries, blue as the sea, yet they picture themselves ending their lives in a kind of picture postcard.

They don't realize that, outside, it's been years since anyone has sent postcards.

Who's going to give you your interferon shots, at the beach?

I have more respect for someone who tells me: I'm going to the mountains, even though he's never been there and doesn't know what it's like. But he says: I want to stay in the mountains until all the noise I've soaked up over these years gets out of my head. Afterwards he doesn't do it, but it doesn't matter.

As for me, I think about finding a middle ground: I'd like to go to the coast, but up north.

Many years ago, on the radio, I heard about a place where every summer, for generations, everyone has gone around naked. You can't go swimming, it's too cold, but it doesn't matter. There are no insects, and the light dies late. You can be by yourself if you want, in company if you like. The people are little black dots on the sand. The sky is high above. You can climb up to the sky and come back down, and it takes quite a bit of time.

Naked not to be searched, or probed. Naked of your own free will. If someone comes up to you, you don't have to ask yourself: I wonder what he's hiding . . . Who knows if it's something that can hurt me. Naked without shame. And without remorse. Able to look without having to cover your eyes. How it hurts, during transfers, to look at women. At tram stops, on balconies, coming out of shops, crossing the street. They pop up from the ground, fly through the air, like pollen. A beauty that burns your eyes. They flourish, unaware of you. But you look just the same. You don't look at the horizon, you look at them. And you're thankful for your escort. And the grilles at the windows, which make it difficult to focus, and make you nauseous. And a siren that shrieks above your head, and makes you pass them quickly.

Up north, where everyone is naked, there'll be no need for it.

The only thing I'll wear is my denture, because in such a beautiful place I want to have teeth. Up there I'll want as much beauty as possible. And there will be gorgeous girls, without make-up, and I'll be able to look at them—being a ghost, I'll be able to look at them exactly the way the young men sitting next to them do, guys younger than the years I've served.

A place full of grace. Of undeserved splendor. Of pardon, finally.

White canvas mounted on posts, to protect the skin from the sun. Wind that stirs the canvas, the same wind that here makes the cell doors and gates slam. Steps that can't be heard, because of the sand. And under the sand a little warmth, even on the chilliest days. On crystalline days I'll watch the ice floes, across the sea, and in winter I'll even cross them. Because it's not true that there is no work suitable for a former lifer, and that the world is closed to him, more sealed than prison. There are jobs that are perfect for us. In the world of glaciers, scientists lose their minds, shut up in twelve-by-twelve-foot labs, while outside it's perpetually cold and dark. They become aggressive, paranoid, delirious, depressed in the polar night. When the wind dies down, they hear the creaking of the ice. It sounds like footsteps, but it's cracks: it's the sea, beneath, tossing about. And although the ice is more than a mile thick, the sea below is two and a half miles deep. And it heaves. The solid fresh water floats on the salty seawater, inhabited by creatures that no one has ever seen, that have no name. Even robots break down, at certain temperatures. I cost less than a robot, and I'm used to the cold, the dark. Used to solitude. The scientists can stay on their campuses and tell me what to do. I have no problem taking orders.

I'm *patient.*

If they go to the ice fields to study the world's past, along with its illnesses, viruses that have been hibernating, I'm the right person to assist them. I know what an infection lasting ten or a hundred thousand years is like. And if the melting ice masses liberate the future earth, I'm the right person. Past and future. Never mind the present. I'm not even hungry anymore. What matters is that every spring they let me return to the beach, across the sea.

Fires. Maybe some have stayed.

Pillowcases, towels, t-shirts, strips of cloth burning, hung from the gratings, as if to dry. It's not a conflagration, you don't see any outstretched arms, only flames. They've lit fires. A glow, even down here. No flame higher than the perimeter wall. Invisible from outside, from the town.

If it were an uprising all the tiers would have been lit up or all dark. Instead, each cell seems to have acted on its own. And this silence, more inexplicable than the big light being out, and the small fires they've lit. The prison's loculi, with their small lamps. The obsession with fire. Because a fire makes you forget the cold, the feeling of emptiness inside you, of damp, bare cells that transmit the chill. A bonfire: I'm setting fire to ten years of my life. I'm setting fire to the time that separates me from an afterwards, from outside. There is no revolt without a fire, because inmates overestimate the prison, they think it's more impregnable than it is. If it can crush me, if it can prostrate me, if I am nothing in its eyes, it's because it is invincible. I can do anything to it without really hurting it: let's set fires!

But it's not so.

I know of a prison where at the visits, during the holiday season, they authorized centerpiece candles, but no one noticed that they had a paper base. They forgot them there, leaving them burning!!! Or maybe they didn't feel like putting them out. Maybe it seemed inauspicious, who knows, to blow out the candles before leaving the visiting room. As if there were nothing left to stay there for. Neither the inmates nor the guards blew the candles out. They left the room without looking back and the candles, as they burned down, ignited the paper. The small plastic tables melted and shrivelled up. As did the plastic of the white and red chairs. The ludicrous material of the chairs of those absent from home. The rancor, secreted on so many nights, absorbed by the mattresses, by foam rubber so thin that outside they wouldn't even use it for packing. The air becomes saturated, old prisons aren't equipped to discharge smoke and heat. There are heavy cell doors and sally ports to prevent the living from moving, but no fire doors. The extinguishers are empty, the electrical system isn't up to code, the water supply is dependent upon the city. And if the city, for whatever reason, shuts off the water, the prison burns. There's no emergency lighting either. At a time like this those lights should be on, but the corridor is pitch black, impenetrable. Evacuating a burning prison in the dark is hell. Hell on earth. Commander wrote to the administration, but as far as I know, no one ever responded. Commander also spoke about it with Toro and with the family from the North: Tell your guys to be careful, if this prison burns no one will put the fire out. And with the heat the locks will fuse. With the heat the guards won't be able to open up even if they wanted to . . .

I hope it continues like this, with small fires out there under the sky.

In all the uprisings they set fire, but this isn't an uprising. It would be an odd time. Uprisings start out in the yard, or at meals, not in the final hours of the night when we're locked up, when they only open the cells for emergencies, individually.

This is not an uprising.

It's nothing. Nothing at all. As if the prison had already burned down, and those fires were the last embers.

People walk around during an uprising. They spend hours walking around. Looking for someone and not finding him, because everyone is walking around. You enjoy moving about so much that you don't think about escaping anymore. You walk around, wreck things, eat, some people make love, some get knifed, most guys go up and down the corridors with cloths over their heads, so they won't be recognized. As if the prison had suddenly become as big as the world, and you didn't know who lived there and who didn't. You go to the infirmary to get some alcohol for bottle bombs, or for drinking, you get a supply of psychotropic drugs. Some, many, run to the storerooms and steal more food than they can ever eat. Everyone rips the wiring out of the walls, the pipes, looking for the prison's veins in the concrete and throwing them into the corridor. They tear out the sinks, the light switches, pull down the cots. The prison fills with burning cloth and water pouring in. They knock over the lockers. It's your home and you destroy it; you'll suffer for it. That makes you rage even more. You know that when the guards retake the prison you'll sleep on the ground, you won't get any food, and then you'll travel for hours without knowing where they're taking you. You destroy it anyway. Someone else will gain by rebuilding it, you lose by destroying it. Each cell finds, within itself, the means to tear itself to pieces. Only those who haven't known rage can be amazed at how easily doors and gates come down. The rage that accumulates when you sleep for years, locked up, beside others who sleep with rage. A surge of rage that cleanses, sweeps away thought, revives the circulation. A surge of rage to ride like a wave, trying to stay up as long as possible, before being knocked down.

Only the new prisons are able to defend themselves on their own, the old ones keep us locked up so that we will acquiesce. When you stop working together, a swollen river washes over everything. You find people and things in the yard that moments before were on the tiers. That river, on the island, even reached me, 1,532 days after I had killed the guard. Ten days of uninterrupted darkness, 1,522 days of lights constantly on, though I was unable to count them, since they brought me food at odd times. They came to free me at seven in the evening, and I was sure it was morning. Suddenly free. In prison, on the island, but free.

When the others climbed up to the roof, I stayed in the yard.

They went up because that was what they did in those years. With the low roofs, and emptiness all around, it didn't make much sense. It makes sense in the city: you climb up and people applaud from the square. From nearby houses, photographers shoot their pictures with telephoto lenses as long as cannons. Even a guy who goes around wearing a mask takes it off on the roofs. He thinks: They can't kill me as long as someone sees me. In the city, during uprisings, the prisoners demand to speak with magistrates and journalists but most of all photographers. At one time reaching the roofs was easy. There were projecting moldings that could be dug out to from handholds. Now they've reinforced them throughout. Tired of having people up there. On the island there were no journalists, no magistrates, no houses or squares; the inmates sat astride the roof because it was nice up there. Not to put up banners or pull off roof tiles. Straddling it: one leg north, one south. One east, one west. One to the sea, one to the mountains, one up one down, one secure one free . . . it expands the horizon a hundredfold. You sense that the prison is ready. It's trembling with impatience. It's tired of standing there, rotting. If you prick it, it might burst. You can make it leap over the wall, in its entirety, with its tiers, its basements, its beams. Only the records office and the guards' barracks will be left inside the walls, because they don't have anyone riding astride them. Which actually isn't true . . . because even the guards are glad to climb up on the rooftops. They scrutinize the area with telescopic rifles or they come, in anti-riot gear, to drag down the rebellious ones. Then once their work is done they stay longer than necessary. They too sit there with their legs spread out, as if they were on an excursion in the mountains; with the panoramic view, and the satisfaction of taking off their boots and resting on the summit.

During an uprising rumors fly.

On the second day they said that a team of crack sharpshooters had arrived from the mainland, with military rifles capable of striking miles away. And that the political prisoners were already negotiating their release in exchange for a statement, to be published in all the newspapers. They also said that a snitch had been decapitated, and that they had played ball with his head before throwing it over the wall. But when I saw the body, it was still attached. A head is as hard as a rock, and doesn't roll easily. Its trajectories are unpredictable, it decides if it will keep moving straight toward the door, or if it will turn away in the end, tracing circles.

No one ever saw the body of that informer again. Who for that matter wasn't the biggest snitch of all, on that island of informers. He was just the most disliked. They body was sent to the mainland, for the autopsy, and we lost track of him. At one time inmates' corpses belonged to the state, which could transfer them dead just as it moved them around when alive; it could donate them to a university or burn them, without having to ask anyone's permission. If the state didn't want them, they belonged to the family members. And if the family members weren't interested either, they were buried near the prison, in a cemetery for deceased individuals who won't be receiving any visitors.

Piscio was buried that way, since there was a cemetery here too, once. They dug it up ten years ago, to expand the guards' parking lot. It was well situated, like most cemeteries by the sea. Better than in the town square. The guards never had a cemetery, and if you ask me, they enjoyed taking ours away.

On the third day they agreed to sell me and they began to 'pamper' me.

'Pamper' is a technical term that wasn't used at the time. The N's use it now, when the victim is one of theirs, and they need to shower him with attentions so that he'll lower his guard. So he won't disappear, won't scream, and will let himself be led to the slaughterhouse without making a fuss.

The most humane way to slaughter animals, which is also the way to ensure that the meat stays firm and doesn't darken when it's cut, or become mushy, the most humane way is to make them go through a narrow, curving chute. With no whistling or shouting. A chute with a level floor, with no glittering puddles or forgotten cloths left on the walls by slaughterhouse attendants. The chute must limit the animals' vision and make them feel they're with others. Most of all: it must create the sensation of returning to the starting point. Animals move willingly if they think they're going back to the truck they got out of. They go willingly from dark to light, provided the sun isn't in their eyes. A diffuse, indirect light, to shroud the butchery. Meat without stress.

The N's 'pamper' those they have to kill.

And who better than friends can do that? That's one of the bad things about organizations: you're forced to kill people with whom you grew up. But it's also the beauty of them. I know of an informer, one of the N's, a young man who was placed under protection in a hotel, far away from everyone, with guards who passed by once a day, for five minutes, just to fill up his fridge. It was a mistake. The trial took forever to start, and he ended up phoning his old buddies. Because he knew that they would 'pamper' him. He had a desperate need to have fun, that kid.

I didn't have any buddies, so they all 'pampered' me a little. Even Toro pampered me.

They pampered me even though there was no need. Where could I escape to? Who would hear me scream? Who cared about what my hide was worth? They pampered me out of inertia. And because by then the uprising was almost at an end, the yard littered with trash, the air dense with tear gas, one-million-candle-power spotlights, the deafening bursts of grenades and the whistling in the ears afterwards, and even later on, for hours, the drone of the army's generators and the beams of the searchlights. They let me fall asleep and lowered me over the wall as I slept. I woke up encircled by the guards, surrounded by the dogs.

I don't know what they promised the ones who sold me. I know that to the guards I was more important than anyone else. Anyone else could get away, or die, not me. They wanted me for all time, because I had killed one of their own. They didn't beat me either. They beat my companions a whole lot more, later on, despite the promises. They weren't angry with me. I was simply something returned to them.

A prison is truly new only if you can manage it all remotely, Commander explained to me. When I go to the capital, he said, they ask me: Aren't you fed up with watching ageing assholes? Of searching the same inmate a thousand, a hundred thousand times, over the years? In the new prisons, almost always empty, they move prisoners on paved roads. No perimeter wall, only fencing.

Here the walls are rotten, Commander said. The inmates dig them out with teaspoons because they were built with teaspoons, that's how closely packed the earth was. In the new ones there are only high-tension steel wires, razor sharp and alarmed. You need land for a new-generation prison, acreage that costs little, you can't mistake it for a castle, or a monastery, because it never was one. Viewed from above it looks like markings for fields, airports. Video cameras, wires, and that's all; guards need walls to walk on, and the new prisons are so huge that dogs can't patrol them. Beyond the fencing, water and fuel storage, a highway interchange. The parking lot. And beyond that, more barrenness. Forest, maybe, or desert. Overhead: restricted air space. In the new prisons nobody walks. There are no windows large enough to allow a body to pass through, and therefore no need for bars or for checking them, rattling them to ensure that they're intact. Glass serves to keep out sounds. And when a prisoner must be moved, he does it on his own, in a sealed segment of the prison, with no chance of assaulting or talking to anyone, and therefore with no need to be searched: if he behaves correctly, the next segment will open, otherwise it remains shut; gas is then introduced, and a team intervenes. The heavy keys attached to the belt, clanging up and down the stairs, are no longer needed. Only magnets. As long as the current passes through them they cling together so forcefully that it's impossible to separate them; turning off the power, they open up.

A prison could be beautiful, Commander murmured to me. A place of silence, of serenity.

The beds, concrete, all one with the wall.

Concrete shelves. A concrete chair, a concrete table, a container for personal items also of concrete. Disorder is impossible, discord is impossible, in a space where nothing can be moved.

Why kill, sacrifice, if there are no boundary markers?

Prison isn't meant to return someone to the world. Its purpose is to seal the wound, cover it over, form a scar. It can seal it up in an unwholesome, chaotic way, or in a sterile, appropriate way. The only truly pitiful city: Pompeii.

Have you been there? I asked Commander.

Where?

Pompeii.

There's so much more peace and dignity in the new prisons, he insisted, leaning against the slot in my cell door, no more guards to bribe or informers to court. If you behave well, your meal will be slightly better each day, your phone calls more frequent. The air in the cell will have a fresher smell, a more intense, more varied zest. You're alone, but you eat. No more arbitrary abuse. No more empty time, the same for everyone, filled with harassment. No false testimony, because there is nothing to testify to. And what little there may be is recorded by the cameras.

On some points I even thought he was right. But I sensed that he was beginning to feel tired. Like me.

Where would you walk at night? I asked him. And where would they get the money? Even if they managed to build it, they would end up overcrowding it, as they've always done, until it was overwhelmed.

We talked about many of those things, on many of those nights . . . I never really took Commander seriously when he talked about the new prison. Only when strange things began to happen, when I stopped understanding the prison and Commander stopped coming down, only then did I begin to think back. To feel uneasy.

On one of the last nights, toward morning, when they'd already opened up the tiers and we heard the attendants come down, dragging the milk cans into the kitchen, and sweeping the concrete in the yard, he said to me: When I was little they used to take me fishing, and I would look down from the boat and wish that all the water would disappear. So I could see the fish clearly. Make out where they were going, what they were doing, what they were hiding from me.

I remember a film, a submarine stranded on the bottom of the ocean. At first, the crew stopped talking and cooking, to conserve oxygen, but later, realizing there was really nothing more that could be done, they relit all the candles on the Christmas tree and sang together. It's the kind of movie they show during the holidays, to make you feel fortunate. In another movie an astronaut wakes up halfway into the journey. I don't remember if it was because of something that went wrong or the result of someone's vicious act: he was supposed to sleep for thousands of years and instead he woke up, with all that emptiness around him. His companions sleeping peacefully, enclosed in their pods. I don't know what sounds you hear in a spaceship of the future: I imagine silence. At most a hum, a vibration. On the island sometimes the silence was so intense that I would scrape my fingernail against the bar of the bed to make sure that I hadn't gone deaf. Either too much noise or too much silence. I don't even remember how the movie ended, whether the astronaut let himself die of hunger and thirst or was able to kill himself first, with what little can be found in a spaceship. Whether he wrote something on the walls, for his companions to find when they awoke. Or for aliens, anyone. Or maybe he tried to wake everyone up, even knowing he'd be condemning them. Maybe he ordered the computer to do it, and then ran to his pod, the coward, pretending that he too woke up that same moment. Or possibly he pressed their buttons, one by one, looking each one in the eye and saying: I woke you up, because I couldn't stand being alone.

That's how the need to talk works. You think: if I talk, they'll beat me and throw buckets of water at me in the dark, making it impossible for me to sleep . . . Or they'll tie me up on the ground, arms and legs spread out. But it doesn't matter, I'll talk just the same. I'll take the chance. And the man in the cell next to yours usually takes the chance as well, he doesn't deny you those few measly words.

Here we're more fortunate. No one harms us if we talk. It's solitary, in a manner of speaking. Water flows in the pipes and air filters through, in this poorly sealed prison. There are also insects, more and more of them since the attendants disappeared. Drinking the water in the dark, it seems full of insects. I heard on the radio that humanity must learn to eat them, in order to survive. It's just a stupid cultural taboo. You find insects after any catastrophe. But it may take a while between the time man vanishes and they arrive. I don't think there are enough of them here now, to feed us, I mean. Then too, if we start eating them, they might leave. Crawl away, if they can't fly. They can pass under the reinforced door. I on the other hand find it hard to breathe, regardless of the chinks. Even during the worst of the isolation periods, they'd throw food at you every now and then. They'd

come to beat me. Maybe they sold it, this old irre-
deemable prison, and forgot to take us out. You always
forget something, in a move. It's harder to forget the
managers, or the guards . . . Maybe before long they'll
send builders to work here. Less than a year. But not
soon enough. Or maybe, simply, a hurricane is coming,
in this sea that's usually so small and contained. They
evacuated everyone. Almost everyone. And the hurricane will blow away the stones carried up by the juvenile offenders a hundred years ago, so that the builders
who come afterwards will be able to ignore the footprint
of the old prison; they'll be able to focus solely on the
new hotel, and it will turn out better.

When Commander spoke to me about the new
prison I would tell him: There will never be enough
space here, even if they wanted to. If we tear down the
old one, they'll build a hotel. Is that what you want? Do
you want tourists strolling through the corridors where
we walked?

I wonder if anyone is watching us.

From the corners maybe, some video cameras capable of seeing in the dark.

Or a satellite in the sky at least, has it noticed that
the big orange light is out?

I hope someone has noticed it. And decides to come
back.

I pray that Toro, the N's, Commander, the guards are
looking for one another now, armed, in the dark, to
harm each other. I pray they're silent for that reason.
Now I know how the Princess felt, the night I returned

late. The fear of dying in shackles: not killed, left to die. Because if someone is looking for you, you can always hope to get away, overpower him, or move him to pity. The beauty of a death that comes by someone else's hand is that it leaves you hope of getting off scot-free. You're under the illusion that if you save yourself from a violent death, normal death will forget about you. But if no one is looking for you, you have to resign yourself to the fact that you will vanish. And the houses where you lived will crumble into dust. Even this one, which is the sturdiest house of all, a house built to endure. And one day a fire will destroy the record books where your name was written, and then there will really be nothing left, not even your crimes; and I'm not ready for that.

ACKNOWLEDGMENTS

My thanks to: Nino B., Ilaria Caretta, Lucia Castellano, Marta Costantino, Paola Gallo, and Marco Peano.

As well as to: Jack Henry Abbot, Riccardo Arena, Libero Ballinari, Roberto Bezzi, Chris Blatchford, Alfredo Bozzi, Malcolm Braly, James H. Bruton, Edward Bunker, Don Carpenter, Cesare Casella, Stefania Chiusoli, Ted Conover, Daniela De Robert, Pete Earley, Ornella Favero, Bruce Franklin, Prospero Gallinari, Jack London, Norman Mailer, Gigi Moncalvo, Giuliano Naria, Charlie Norman, Giorgio Panizzari, Antonio Perrone, Manuel Puig, Emilio Quadrelli, Aldo Ricci, Giulio Salierno, Goliarda Sapienza, Pino Scaccia, Giuseppe Soffiantini, Donatella Tesi, and William R. Wilkinson.

www.mauriziotorchio.com